TURTLE MOUNTAIN TALES

and Other Band of Chippewa Folklore

By

Brittany Hamley

Copyright © 2024 Brittany Hamley

The right of Brittany Hamley to be identified as author of this work has been asserted by the author in accordance with sections 77 and 78 of the Copyright, Designs and Patents Act 1988. All rights reserved. No part of this publication may be reproduced, distributed, or transmitted in any form or by any means, including photocopying, recording, or other electronic or mechanical methods, without the prior written permission of the publishers. Any person who commits any unauthorized act in relation to this publication may be liable to criminal prosecution and civil claims for damages. This is a work of fiction. Names, characters, businesses, places, events, locales, and incidents are either the products of the author's imagination or used in a fictitious manner. Any resemblance to actual persons, living or dead, or actual events is purely coincidental.

ISBN: 9798876501738 (Paperback)

Front cover image by Brittany Hamley.

Book design by Brittany Hamley.

Printed by Kindle Direct Publishing.

Sold and Shipped from Amazon.com.

First printing edition 2024.

Illustrations Copyright: Public Domain. We have determined this work to be in the public domain, meaning that it is not subject to copyright. Users are free to copy, use, and redistribute the work in part or in whole. http://publicdomainvectors.org

Photographs Copyright: Public Domain We have determined this work to be in the public domain, meaning that it is not subject to copyright. Users are free to copy, use, and redistribute the work in part or in whole. Courtesy of Turtle Mountain Chippewa Heritage Center.

TABLE OF CONTENTS

INTRODUCTION	13
CHIPPEWA TRADITIONS	23
NANABOSHO	27
THE ORIGIN OF INDIAN CORN	33
THE CREATION STORY	39
TURTLE ISLAND	45
GREAT SERPENT AND THE GREAT FLOOD	51
HOW DOGS CAME TO THE INDIANS	57
THE ORIGIN OF THE BIG DIPPER	61
THEFT OF FIRE	67
THE DREAM FAST	71
MANABOZHO'S ADVENTURES	77
MANABOZHO AND THE MAPLE TREES	83
THE GIRLS WHO WISHED TO MARRY STARS	89
WENEBOJO AND THE WOLVES	93
WENEBOJO AND THE WORLD	99
WENEBOJO AND THE MOOSE'S SKULL	103
WENEBOJO AND THE CRANBERRIES	107
WENEBOJO AND THE DANCING GEESE	109
WINDIGO	113
ANOTHER WINDIGO STORY	117
THE UNDERWATER PANTHER	119

THE MINK AND THE FISH 123
THE HELLDIVER AND THE SPIRIT OF
WINTER 125
THE STORY OF REDFEATHER 129
WHY THE PORCUPINE HAS QUILLS 133
WHY THE BUFFALO HAS A HUMP 135
WENEBOJO MADE A HOUSE FOR TORTOISE
.... 137
THE MAGIC POTS 141
HOW THE INDIANS GOT MAPLE SUGAR ... 145
SKUNK WOMAN 147
SHAWONDASEE AND THE GOLDEN GIRL . 151
OLD MAN REMAKES THE WORLD 153
HOW THE MAN FOUND HIS MATE 163

Dedicated to my Father-in-law,

I may not have given you grandkids, but I refuse to let your heritage die with me.

INTRODUCTION

The Chippewas are one of the largest American Indian groups in North America. There are nearly 150 different bands of Chippewa Indians living throughout their original homeland in the northern United States (especially North Dakota, Minnesota, Wisconsin, and Michigan) and southern Canada (especially Ontario, Manitoba, and Saskatchewan.) Each Ojibwe community lives on its own reservation (or reserve, in Canada). Reservations are lands that belong to the Ojibwes and are under their control. Communities of Ojibwe Indians are called tribes in the United States and First Nations in Canada. Each Ojibwe tribe is politically independent and has its own government, laws, police, and services, just like a small country. Some Ojibwe nations have also formed coalitions to address common problems.

The political leader of an Ojibway band is called a chief (*gimaa* or *ogimaa* in the Ojibway language.) In the past Ojibway chiefs were men chosen by tribal councilmembers, often from among the last chief's sons, nephews, or sons-in-law. Today Ojibway chiefs can be men or women, and they are elected in most Ojibway bands, like mayors and governors. Ojibwe comes from an Algonquian word meaning 'puckered,' probably because of the tribe's distinctive puckered style of shoes. The pronunciation is like *o-jib-way*, but many native speakers pronounce the first syllable very short or even drop it, which is why it sounded like "Chippewa" to some colonists. The Ojibway people also call themselves Anishinabe in their own language, which means 'original person.' What is the difference between Chippewa, Ojibway, Ojibwe, and Ojibwa? There is no difference. All these different spellings refer to the same people. In the United States more people use 'Chippewa,' and in Canada more people use 'Ojibway,' but all four of these spellings are common. Since the Ojibwe language did not originally have its own alphabet, spellings of Ojibwe words in English can sometimes vary a lot, and most people use them interchangeably.

Most Ojibway people speak English, but some of them also speak their native Ojibway language. Ojibway is a musical language that has complicated verbs with many parts. If you'd like to know a few easy Ojibway words, *aaniin* (pronunciation ah-neen) means "hello" and *miigwech* (pronunciation mee-gwetch) means "thank you." Ojibwe is spoken over a broad range in both Canada and the United States, and so there are multiple dialects of the language. The pronunciation guide above is based on Southern Ojibwe (the dialect spoken in North Dakota, where the Turtle Mountain Band of Chippewa are based.) However, Ojibwe vowels are pronounced a little differently in the different dialects. In Ottawa, for example, aw is pronounced the same as ow, like the "ow" in "bowl." In Northern Ojibwe, there's no pronunciation difference between g and k at the beginning of a word. In both Eastern Ojibwe and Ottawa, unstressed short vowels are not pronounced at all, so the word *makak* is pronounced 'mkak' in Eastern Ojibwe, or the word *mashkodiisimin* is pronounced 'mskodiismin'. There are many other examples of dialect differences between Ojibwe communities.

Ojibway women were farmers and did most of the childcare and cooking. Men were hunters and sometimes went to war to protect their families. Both genders practiced storytelling, artwork and music, and traditional medicine. Ojibway men and women worked together to harvest wild rice. An Ojibway man used a pole to steer through the reeds, while his wife knocked rice grains into the canoe. Some Ojibway people still use canoes for ricing today. There were two types of dwellings used by the Chippewas. In the woodlands, Ojibway people lived in villages of birchbark houses called *waginogans*, or wigwams. On the Great Plains, the Ojibwas lived in large buffalo-hide tents called tipis. The Plains Ojibwa were nomadic people, and tipis (or tepees) were easier to move from place to place than a *waginogan*. Here are some pictures of wigwam, tipi, and other Indian houses. Today, Native Americans only build a wigwam or tepee for fun or to connect with their heritage, not as shelter. Most Ojibways live in modern houses and apartment buildings, just like you.

The most important Chippewa trading partners were other Chippewas. There were many different Ojibway bands, and they were closely allied with each other. The Chippewa Indians were also allies with their nearest kinfolk, the Ottawa, and Potawatomi tribes. The Ottawa, Potawatomi, and Ojibway tribes called themselves the Council of Three Fires. The Ojibway tribe frequently fought with rivals like the Iroquois and the Sioux tribes.

Chippewa women wore long dresses with removable sleeves. Chippewa men wore breechcloths and leggings. Everybody wore moccasins on their feet and cloaks or ponchos in bad weather. Later, the

Chippewas adapted European costume such as cloth blouses and jackets, decorating them with fancy beadwork. Here are more pictures of Ojibway clothing styles, and some photographs and links about Native American clothes in general. Traditionally, the Chippewas wore leather headbands with feathers standing straight up in the back. In times of war, some Chippewa men shaved their heads in the Mohawk style, with a single strip of hair standing up high in the middle of the man's head. Otherwise, Chippewa men and women both wore their hair in long braids. A Chippewa warrior might wear a porcupine roach, which you can still see today at pow-wows. In the 1800's, some Chippewa chiefs began wearing long headdresses like their neighbors the Dakota Sioux. Here are some pictures of these different styles of Native American headdress. The Chippewas painted their faces and arms with bright colors for special occasions. They used different patterns for war paint and festive decoration. Some Chippewas, especially men, also wore tribal tattoos.

The Ojibway Indian tribe was well-known for their birchbark canoes. Canoeing is still popular in the Ojibway nation today, though few people handcraft their own canoe from birch bark anymore. Here is a website of birchbark canoe pictures. Over land, Chippewa people used dogs as pack animals. (There were no horses in North America until colonists brought them over from Europe.) The Chippewas used sleds and snowshoes to help them travel in the winter.

Ojibway bands lived in different environments, so they didn't all eat the same types of foods. Woodland Chippewas were mostly farming people, harvesting wild rice and corn, fishing, hunting small game, and gathering nuts and fruit. Here is a website about Ojibwe wild rice. The Plains Ojibwa were big-game hunters, and bison meat made up most of their diet.

Ojibway warriors used bows and arrows, clubs, flails, and hide shields. Hunters also used snares to catch birds, and when Plains Ojibway men hunted buffalo, they often set controlled fires to herd the animals into traps or over falls. Chippewas used spears or fishhooks with sinew lines for fishing, and special paddles called knockers for ricing.

Ojibway artists are known for their beautiful bead embroidery, particularly floral design. Other traditional Ojibway crafts include Native American baskets and birch bark boxes. Like other eastern American Indians, the Ojibways also crafted wampum out of white and purple shell beads. Wampum beads were traded as a kind of currency, but they were more culturally important as an art material. The symbols and designs on wampum belts often told a story or represented a person's family.

Captivating traditions have been passed down through Chippewa generations, captivating and seamlessly blending ancient wisdom with contemporary relevance. Holding a rich tapestry of history, culture, and spirituality, these traditions are deeply rooted in the beliefs and practices of the Chippewa people, also known as the Ojibwe or Anishinaabe. Inhabiting the Great Lakes regions for centuries, from their sacred ceremonies to their connection with nature, the Chippewa traditions offer a glimpse into a world that is both fascinating and profound. Exploration of the Chippewa traditions uncovers the timeless teachings that hold immense value in today's fast-paced world. The enduring legacy of the Chippewa people extends far beyond ancestral, lands and resonates with those who seek a deeper understanding of themselves and the world. Discover the beauty, wisdom, and significance of Chippewa traditions and delve into their customs, stories, and rituals that continue to shape their vibrant culture.

Chippewa traditions have faced numerous challenges over centuries, causing frustrations and concerns among community members. A key issue revolving around the preservation of cultural practices and customs. With the increasing influence of Western culture, Chippewa traditions have been slowly eroding. Many are left feeling a sense of loss and disconnection from their ancestral heritage. As outside forces encroach upon and disrupt not only the balance of nature but has also threatened the very foundations of Chippewa identity and spirituality. The lack of recognition and respect for Chippewa traditions from mainstream society has perpetuated a cycle of marginalization and discrimination, making it difficult for the community to thrive and flourish. These issues pose significant obstacles to the preservation of Chippewa traditions, threatening the community's sense of identity and spirituality. By shedding light on these injustices and sharing traditional stories of folklore, we can continue to keep their existence alive, proud, and loud.

At the heart of the Chippewa traditions lies a profound spiritual connection to nature. The Chippewa people believe that all living things possess a spirit and that everything in the world is interconnected. These beliefs are reflected in their rituals, ceremonies, and daily practices. Tribes live in harmony with the environment and with the respect for the delicate balance of ecosystems.

The Chippewa have a wide range of sacred traditional practices that are the soul of their cultural identity, including storytelling, music, dance, and art. These practices serve as a vital means of transmitting their history, values, and wisdom to younger generations. Storytelling provides a platform for passing down historical events, legends, and moral teachings. Elder members of the community play a crucial role in the preservation of this oral tradition, ensuring that stories are accurately retold and shared. Music and dance hold high significant importance in Chippewa celebrations and ceremonies. The two most important Ojibwe instruments are the drum and the flute. Ojibwe drums were usually large, and several men would play them together at tribal festivals and ceremonies. Flutes were carved from wood were most often used to play love songs. Drumming is a fundamental element, with the beat symbolizing the heartbeat of the earth. Traditional dances, such as the Jingle Dance, Hoop Dance, and Fancy Shawl Dance, not only serve as forms of artistic expression but also as ways to honor ancestors connecting with them in the spiritual realm. Renowned for their craftsmanship and artistic talents like beadwork, birch bark biting, and quillwork, these intricate designs and patterns carefully preserved over time serve as visual representations of cultural heritage and are often incorporated into clothing, accessories, and other décor.

One of the primary objectives of Chippewa traditions is to pass down knowledge and values from one generation to the next. The tribe places great emphasis on intergenerational learning, recognizing the importance of preserving their cultural heritage through education and mentorship. Elders play a vital role in this process, as they possess a wealth of wisdom and experience. They act as teachers and mentors, guiding younger members of the community in understanding and embracing Chippewa traditions. Through storytelling, hands-on learning, and shared experiences, elders impart valuable lessons on spirituality, respect for nature, and community values. Chippewa youth are encouraged to actively participate in cultural activities from birth, learning traditional songs, dances, and crafts while fostering a sense of pride and identity within their cultural roots. Schools and community centers provide formal education ensuring that the younger generation can continue to carry these traditions forward.

Throughout history, the Chippewa have faced numerous challenges and adversities, including colonization, forced assimilation, and the encroachment of their ancestral lands. Despite these hardships, they have demonstrated remarkable resilience in preserving their traditions and adapting to changing circumstances. Chippewa communities have actively engaged in cultural revitalization efforts, establishing language immersion programs, cultural centers, and powwows. These initiatives serve as platforms for fostering cultural pride, strengthening community bonds, and ensuring the survival of Chippewa traditions for future generations. The Chippewa have embraced modern technology as a means of preserving their cultural heritage. By utilizing these digital platforms, such as websites and social media, they can share traditions with a broader audience to connect with other indigenous communities worldwide. This adaptation to the digital age reflects the Chippewa's commitment to safeguarding their cultural identity while embracing the opportunities of the present. Through their deep connection to nature, the preservation of traditional practices, and the passing down of knowledge and values, the Chippewa continue to honor their cultural heritage with their ability to adapt and embrace modern tools, ensuring their traditions thrive in an ever-changing world. Recognizing the importance of preserving cultural diversity and fostering respect for indigenous peoples, we can celebrate and learn from their traditions and their invaluable contributions to humanity.

CHIPPEWA TRADITIONS

The Chippewa, also known as the Ojibwe or Anishinaabe, are a Native American tribe indigenous to North America with a rich cultural heritage. Known for their strong connection to nature, spirituality, and community, Chippewa traditions encompass a wide range of practices and beliefs that have been passed down through generations, shaping their way of life.

Having a deep reverence for the natural world and spiritual belief in the interconnectedness of all living beings is one of the key aspects of Chippewa traditions and their spiritual beliefs. The Chippewa believe that everything in natural has a spirit, and they strive to maintain a harmonious relationship with the land, water, plants, and animals. This belief system is reflected in their rituals, ceremonies, and daily practices. Ceremonies play a significant role in Chippewa traditions. They hold various ceremonies throughout the year to honor the changing season, celebrate harvest, and mark important life events. The most well-known ceremonies is that of the powwow, which brings together different tribes to showcase traditional dances, music, and regalia. Chippewa traditions also emphasize the importance of community and kinship. Extended family networks are highly values, and decisions are often made collectively. The tribe has a strong sense of communal responsibility, where individuals are expected to contribute to the well-being of the community. This includes sharing resources, supporting each other in times of need, and participating in community events.

Additionally, storytelling is an integral part of Chippewa traditions. Elders pass down oral histories, legends, and myths that teach moral lessons and preserve their cultural identity. These stories often feature animal spirits, heroic figures, and mythical creatures, providing a deeper understanding of the Chippewa worldview and their relationship with the spiritual realm.

Included in the vast list of traditions is that of smudging. Smudging is a ritual where sacred herbs, such as sage or sweetgrass, are burned to purify a space or an individual. It is believed to cleanse negative energy and promote spiritual balance. Also included is wild rice harvesting. Wild rice holds significant cultural and economic value for the Chippewa. They have traditional methods of harvesting and processing wild rice, which is considered a sacred food. Dreamcatchers are intricately woven hoops with a web-like structure meant to catch bad dreams and allow good dreams to pass through. They are another tradition and symbol of protection either commonly hung in homes or worn as jewelry. Another tradition is the Medicine Wheel. The Chippewa use the Medicine Wheel as a tool for spiritual guidance and healing. It represents the four directions, elements, seasons, and stages of life, providing framework for understanding the interconnectedness of all things. The Jingle Dress Dance is a traditional dance form originated among the Chippewa and is now performed by many Native American tribes. The dancers wear dresses adorned with metal jingles that create a distinctive sound, believed to have healing properties. These Chippewa traditions are just a glimpse of the rich cultural heritage that has been passed down through generations. They serve as a reminder of the tribe's deep connection to nature, spirituality, and community, shaping their way of life and preserving their identity.

There are many Ojibway legends and fairy tales. Storytelling is very important to the Ojibway Indian culture. Many traditional Ojibway stories taught important lessons to children, while others were just for fun. Here is one legend about the origin of the robin, and another about the creation of the Earth.

NANABOSHO

Before the Chippewas knew the art of fire-making, Nanabozho taught them the art of making hatchets, lances, and arrowpoints. Also known as Nanabush with different spellings such as Nanabozho, Manabozho, Minabozho or even Wenebojo, Nanabosho is a spirit in the Anishinaabe *aadizookaan* (traditional storytelling), particularly among the Ojibwe. Nanabosho is the teacher and the protector of the Anishinabe people, sent by Creator to help the Anishinabe people. Nanabush discovered that people are not easily assisted and resorts to all kinds of tricks and antics to teach people how to behave and how to survive. The stories of his exploits have been passed down orally for thousands of years. Sometimes Nanabosho changes into other forms, such as a rabbit, an owl, a tree, or a rock to help make a point. Other times he puts himself into a humorous situation to make a point. No matter what he does, he is always teaching.

As a trickster figure, it is often Nanabozho's goal to create problems, which often highlight the struggles many Native American's experience. According to Anishinaabe scholar Leanne Simpson, for instance, Nanabush often experiments with capitalistic means. Natives can be greedy, manipulative, and money driven. Because of their worldly desires, chaos often ensues. However, by developing deep relationships with others, Nanabozho becomes more balanced. Furthermore, as Nanabozho becomes more receptive to surroundings, he is able to create the idea of decolonization through learned consent, recognition, and reciprocity. Therefore, the stories of Nanabush are used to guide people through life experiences and teach moral lessons.

Nanabozho is alleged to be the impersonation of life, the active quickening power of life manifested and embodied in the myriad forms of sentient and physical nature. He is said to possess not only the power to live, but also the correlative power of renewing his own life and of quickening and therefore of creating life in others. He impersonates life in an unlimited series of diverse personalities which represent various phases and conditions of life, and the histories of the life and acts of these separate individualities form an entire cycle of myths and traditions which, when compared one with another, are sometimes contradictory and incongruous relating to various objects and subjects in nature. The conception named Nanabozho exercises the diverse functions of many persons, and the likewise suffers their pains and needs. He is this life struggling with the many forms of want, misfortune, and death that come to the dobies and beings of nature.

Having attained the age of manhood, Nanabozho, still feeling deep resentment for the death of his mother at his brother's birth, resolved to avenge her by destroying his brother and her last-born son Chakekenapok. The two brothers grappled and Chakekenapok turned and fled, but Nanabozho pursued him all over the world, finally overtaking and striking him with a deer horn, fracturing pieces from various parts of his body and destroying him by tearing out his entrails. The fragments from Chakekenapok's body became huge rocks, and the masses of flint found in various parts of the world show where the conflicts between the two brothers took place, while his entrails became vines.

Nanabosho and his younger brother Chipiapoos lived together in land far way from mankind. They were noted for excellence of body and beneficence of mind, and for the supreme character of the magic power they possessed. These qualities and attributes excited the bitter antagonism of the evil *manitos*, or spirits, of the air, earth, and waters, who plotted to destroy these two brothers. Nanabozho, who was immune to the effects of bad juju and from whose knowledge nothing was barred, knew their snares and devices and hence eluded and avoided them. He, however, warned Chipiapoos, his less-gifted brother, not to leave their lodge or to separate from him even for a moment. But, one day Chipiapoos ventured out of the lodge and went on the ice of a great lake, where the *manitos* broke the ice, causing Chipiapoos to sink to the bottom of the lake, where his body was hidden by the *manitos*. Upon returning to the lodge, Nanabozho, missing Chipiapoos and surmising his fate, became inconsolable. Everywhere over the face of the earth he sought for him in vain. Then he became enraged and waged relentless war against all *manitos*, wreaking vengeance by precipitating a multitude of them into the abyss of the world. He declared a truce to mourn for his brother, disfiguring his person and covering his head to indicate grief, bitterly weeping, and uttering from time to time the name of the lost and unhappy Chipiapoos. It is said Nanabozho secluded himself for size years in his lodge of mourning. During his truce the evil *manitos*, knowing the unlimited powers of Nanabozho and recollecting the destruction of the vast numbers of *manitos* by their metamorphosis to gratify his anger, consulted together to devise means for pacifying Nanabozho's wrath. Finally, four of the *manitos*, hoary with age and ripe in experience and wisdom, and who had no been parties to the death of Chipiapoos, undertook a mission of pacification. Having built a lodge of condolence near that of Nanabozho, they prepared a feast of welcome including filling a tobacco pipe. The four ambassadors carried bags made from an otter, a lynx, and a beaver, filled with magically potent medicines. Arriving at Nanabozho's lodge, they chanted to him with ceremonial formality their good intentions and kind greetings and asked him to enter his lodge. Moved by these greetings, Nanabozho uncovered his head, washed himself and accompanied them. The *manitos* offered him a cup of purification medicine which Nanabozho took and found himself completely freed from feelings of resentment and melancholy. He became aware that the melancholy, sadness, hatred, and anger that oppressed him gradually left, and those feelings of joy arose in his heart. He joined in the dances and in the chanting; they all ate and smoked together, and Nanabozho expressed thanks to his hosts for initiating him into the mysteries of the grand medicine.

To further show their good will, the *manitos*, by exercise of their magic powers, brought back the missing Chipiapoos, but he was forbidden to enter the lodge. He received a lighted torch through a crack in the walls of the lodge and was required to rule the country of the manes, where he carried the lighted torch with a non-extinguishing flame.

Subsequently, Nanabozho provided each of his family members with a medicine bag full of the grand medicine and charms. He explained that these practices and ceremonies would cure diseases, obtain abundance in fishing and hunting, and gain a completely victory over their enemies.

Some say that Nanabozho created animals for food, and he caused plants and roots to grow whose virtues cure disease and enable the hunter to kill wild animals to drive away famine. These plants he confided to the watchful care of his grandmother, the great-grandmother of humanity, Mesakkummikokwi, and lest man should invoke her in vain she was strictly forbidden ever to leave her lodge. So, when collecting plants, roots, and herbs for their natural and magic virtues, a Chippewa Indian faithfully leaves on the ground hard by the place whence he has taken the root or plant a small offering to Mesakkummikokwi.

It is said that Nanabozho in his many journeys over the earth destroyed many ferocious monsters of land and water whose continued existence would have placed in jeopardy the fate of mankind. It is believed by the faithful that Nanabozho, resting from his toils, dwells on a great island of ice floating on a large sea in the northland, where the seraphim of auroral light keep nightly vigil. It is also believed that should he set foot on the land the world would at once take fire and every living being would share with it a common destruction. As a perversion of an earlier tradition, it is said that Nanabozho has placed four beneficent humanized beings, one at each of the-four cardinal points or world quarters, to aid in promoting the welfare of humanity.

THE ORIGIN OF INDIAN CORN

In times past, a poor Indian was living with his wife and children in a beautiful part of the country. He was not only poor, but inexpert in procuring food for his family, and his children were all too young to give him assistance. Although poor, he was a man of a kind and contented disposition. He was always thankful to the Great Spirit for everything he received. The same disposition was inherited by his eldest son, who had now arrived at the proper age to undertake the ceremony of the Ke-ig-uish-im-o-win, or fast, to see what kind of a spirit his guide and guardian through life would be. Wunzh, for this was his name, had been an obedient boy from his infancy, and was of a pensive, thoughtful, and mild disposition, so that he was beloved by the whole family.

As soon as the first indications of spring appeared, they built him the customary little lodge, at a retired spot some distance from their own, where he would not be disturbed during this solemn rite. In the meantime, he prepared himself, and immediately went into it and commenced his fast. The first few days he amused himself in the mornings by walking in the woods and over the mountains, examining the early plants and flowers, and in this way prepared himself to enjoy his sleep, and, at the same time, stored his mind with pleasant ideas for his dreams. While he rambled through the woods, he felt a strong desire to know how the plants, herbs, and berries grew, without any aid from man, and why it was that some species were good to eat, and others possessed medicinal or poisonous juices.

He recalled these thoughts to mind after he became too languid to walk about and had confined himself strictly to the lodge; he wished he could dream of something that would prove a benefit to his father and family, and to all others. "True!" he thought, "the Great Spirit made all things, and it is to him that we owe our lives. But could he not make it easier for us to get our food, than by hunting animals and taking fish? I must try to find out this in my visions."

On the third day he became weak and faint and kept his bed. He fancied, while thus lying, that he saw a handsome young man coming down from the sky and advancing towards him. He was richly and gaily dressed, having on a great many garments of green and yellow colors, but differing in their deeper or lighter shades. He had a plume of waving feathers on his head, and all his motions were graceful.

"I am sent to you, my friend," said the celestial visitor, "by that Great Spirit who made all things in the sky and on the earth. He has seen and knows your motives in fasting. He sees that it is from a kind and benevolent wish to do good to your people, and to procure a benefit for them, and that you do not seek for strength in war or the praise of warriors. I am sent to instruct you and show you how you can do your kindred good." He then told the young man to arise, and prepare to wrestle with him, as it was only by this means that he could hope to succeed in his wishes. Wunzh knew he was weak from fasting, but he felt his courage rising in his heart, and immediately got up, determined to die rather than fail. He commenced the trial, and, after a protracted effort, was almost exhausted, when the beautiful stranger said, "My friend, it is enough for once; I will come again to try you;" and, smiling on him, he ascended in the air in the same direction from which he came.

The next day the celestial visitor reappeared at the same hour and renewed the trial. Wunzh felt that his strength was even less than the day before, but the courage of his mind seemed to increase in proportion as his body became weaker. Seeing this, the stranger again spoke to him in the same words he used before, adding, "Tomorrow will be your last trial. Be strong, my friend, for this is the only way you can overcome me and obtain the boon you seek." On the third day he again appeared at the same time and renewed the struggle. The poor youth was very faint in body, but grew stronger in mind at every contest, and was determined to prevail or perish in the attempt. He exerted his utmost powers, and after the contest had been continued the usual time, the stranger ceased his efforts and declared himself conquered. For the first time he entered the lodge, and sitting down beside the youth, he began to deliver his instructions to him, telling him in what manner he should proceed to take advantage of his victory.

"You have won your desires of the Great Spirit," said the stranger. "You have wrestled manfully. Tomorrow will be the seventh day of your fasting. Your father will give you food to strengthen you, and as it is the last day of trial, you will prevail. I know this, and now tell you what you must do to benefit your family and your tribe. Tomorrow," he repeated, "I shall meet you and wrestle with you for the last time; and, as soon as you have prevailed against me, you will strip off my garments and throw me down, clean the earth of roots and weeds, make it soft, and bury me in the spot. When you have done this, leave my body in the earth, and do not disturb it, but come occasionally to visit the place, to see whether I have come to life, and be careful never to let the grass or weeds grow on my grave. Once a month cover me with fresh earth. If you follow my instructions, you will accomplish your object of doing good to your fellow-creatures by teaching them the knowledge I now teach you." He then shook him by the hand and disappeared.

In the morning the youth's father came with some slight refreshments, saying, "My son, you have fasted long enough. If the Great Spirit favors you, he will do it now. It is seven days since you have tasted food, and you must not sacrifice your life. The Master of Life does not require that." "My father," replied the youth, "wait till the sun goes down. I have a particular reason for extending my fast to that hour." "Very well," said the old man, "I shall wait till the hour arrives, and you feel inclined to eat."

At the usual hour of the day the sky-visitor returned, and the trial of strength was renewed. Although the youth had not availed himself of his father's offer of food, he felt that new strength had been given to him, and that exertion had renewed his strength and fortified his courage. He grasped his angelic antagonist with supernatural strength, threw him down, took from him his beautiful garments and plume, and finding him dead, immediately buried him on the spot, taking all the precautions he had been told of, and being very confident, at the same time, that his friend would again come to life. He then returned to his father's lodge and partook sparingly of the meal that had been prepared for him. But he never for a moment forgot the grave of his friend.

He carefully visited it throughout the spring, and weeded out the grass, and kept the ground in a soft and pliant state. Very soon he saw the tops of the green plumes coming through the ground; and the more careful he was to obey his instructions in keeping the ground in order, the faster they grew. He was, however, careful to conceal the exploit from his father. Days and weeks had passed in this way. The summer was now drawing towards a close, when one day, after a long absence in hunting, Wunzh invited his father to follow him to the quiet and lonesome spot of his former fast. The lodge had been removed, and the weeds kept from growing on the circle where it stood, but in its place stood a tall and graceful plant, with bright-colored silken hair, surmounted with nodding plumes and stately leaves, and golden clusters on each side. "It is my friend," shouted the lad; "it is the friend of all mankind. It is Mondawmin (the name for corn). We need no longer rely on hunting alone; for, as long as this gift is cherished and taken care of, the ground itself will give us a living." He then pulled an ear. "See, my father," said he, "this is what I fasted for. The Great Spirit has listened to my voice, and sent us something new, and henceforth our people will not alone depend upon the chase or upon the waters."

He then communicated to his father the instructions given him by the stranger. He told him that the broad husks must be torn away, as he had pulled off the garments in his wrestling; and having done this, directed him how the ear must be held before the fire till the outer skin became brown, while all the milk was retained in the grain. The whole family then united in a feast on the newly grown ears, expressing gratitude to the Merciful Spirit who gave it. So, corn came into the world, and has ever since been preserved.

THE CREATION STORY

Long ago, after the Great Mystery, or Kitchi-Manitou, first peopled the earth, the Anishinabe, or Original People, strayed from their harmonious ways and began to argue and fight with one another. Brother turned against brother and soon the Anishinabe were killing one another over hunting grounds and other disagreements. Seeing that harmony, brotherhood, sisterhood, and respect for all living things no longer prevailed on Earth, Kitchi-Manitou decided to purify the Earth. He did this with water.

The water came in the form of a great flood, or mush-ko'-be-wun', upon the Earth destroying the Anishinabe people and most of the animals as well. Only Nanaboozhoo, the central figure in many of the Anishinabe oral traditions, was able to survive the flood, along with a few animals and birds who managed to swim and fly. Nanaboozhoo floated on a huge log searching for land, but none was to be found as the Earth was now covered by the great flood. Nanaboozhoo allowed the remaining animals and birds to take turns resting on the log as well. Finally, Nanaboozhoo spoke.

"I am going to do something," he said. "I am going to swim to the bottom of this water and grab a handful of earth. With this small bit of Earth, I believe we can create a new land for us to live on with the help of the Four Winds and Kitchi-Manitou."

So Nanaboozhoo dived into the water and was gone for a long time. Finally, he surfaced, and short of breath told the animals that the water is too deep for him to swim to the bottom. All were silent. Finally, Mahng, the Loon spoke up. "I can dive under the water for a long way, which is how I catch my food. I will try to make it to the bottom and return with some Earth in my beak."

The Loon disappeared and was gone for a very long time. Surely, thought the others, the Loon must have drowned. Then they saw him float to the surface, weak and nearly unconscious. "I couldn't make it, there must be no bottom to this water," he gasped. Then Zhing-gi-biss, the helldiver came forward and said, "I will try next, everyone knows I can dive great distances." So, the helldiver went under. Again, a very long time passed, and the others thought he was surely drowned. At last, he too floated to the surface. He was unconscious, and not till he came to could he relate to the others that he too was unable to fetch the Earth from the bottom.

Many more animals tried but failed, including Zhon-gwayzh', the mink, and even Mi-zhee-kay", the turtle. All failed and it seemed as though there was no way to get the much-needed Earth from the bottom. Then a soft muffled voice was heard. "I can do it," it spoke softly. At first no one could see who it was that spoke up. Then, the little Wa-zhushk", muskrat stepped forward. "I'll try," he repeated. Some of the other, bigger, more powerful animals laughed at muskrat. Nanaboozhoo spoke up. "Only Kitchi-Manitou can place judgment on others. If muskrat wants to try, he should be allowed to."

So, muskrat dove into the water. He was gone much longer than any of the others who tried to reach the bottom. After a while Nanaboozhoo and the other animals were certain that muskrat had given his life trying to reach the bottom. Far below the water's surface, Muskrat, had in fact reached the bottom. Very weak from lack of air, he grabbed some Earth in his paw and with all the energy he could muster began to swim for the surface. One of the animals spotted Muskrat as he floated to the surface. Nanaboozhoo pulled him up onto the log. "Brothers and sisters," Nanaboozhoo said, "Muskrat went too long without air, he is dead." A song of mourning and praise was heard across the water as Muskrat's spirit passed on to the spirit world. Suddenly Nanaboozhoo exclaimed, "Look, there is something in his paw!" Nanaboozhoo carefully opened the tiny paw. All the animals gathered close to see what was held so tightly there. Muskrat's paw opened and revealed a small ball of Earth. The animals all shouted with joy. Muskrat sacrificed his life so that life on Earth could begin anew.

    Nanaboozhoo took the piece of Earth from Muskrat's paw. Just then, the turtle swam forward and said, "Use my back to bear the weight of this piece of Earth. With the help of Kitchi-Manitou, we can make a new Earth." Nanaboozhoo put the piece of Earth on the turtle's back. Suddenly, the wind blew from each of the Four Directions, the tiny piece of Earth on the turtle's back began to grow. It grew and grew and grew until it formed a mi-ni-si', or island in the water. The island grew larger and larger, but still the turtle bore the weight of the Earth on his back. Nanaboozhoo and the animals all sang and danced in a widening circle on the growing island. After a while, the Four Winds ceased to blow, and the waters became still. A huge island sat in the middle of the water, and today that island is known as North America.

    Traditional Indian people, including the Ojibway, hold special reverence for the turtle who sacrificed his life and made life possible for the Earth's second people. To this day, the Muskrat has been given a good life. No matter that marshes have been drained and their homes destroyed in the name of progress, the Muskrat continues to survive and multiply. The Muskrats do their part today in remembering the great flood; they build their homes in the shape of the little ball of Earth and the island that was formed from it.

Little Shell III

TURTLE ISLAND

The Ojibwa and some other First Nations people, refer to the world as Turtle Island. Different people have different ways of telling the story of how this part of the world was created... by Kitch-Manitou's ability to envision all that was possible and then bring it into being. It's not known where Kitchi-Manitou went after he created the universe and everything in it nor how long he stayed away. But after some time had passed, he decided to drop by to check up on things, so to speak.

On his return he looked around and saw that Mother Earth, Muzzu-Kummik-Quae seemed to be well. The animals that wandered the land, which swam in the seas and flew in the air held each other in balance as did the trees, the grasses and the thorns.

But on closer look, Manitou realized that something else was possible. He had another vision. He realized that there was one more thing that he could create. He could put on the world a special creature who, like himself, could dream. All other animals Manitou had simply "declared" into existence. But he wanted these new beings to be able to have visions - to see new possibilities for themselves and others so he knew he had to pass on his own spiritual essence.

Because commonly spoken of Kitchi Manitou as if he was a person, you may have forgotten that what he is personifying is possibility...the possibility of everything in the universe that we know and everything that we don't know. But there are lesser possibilities. For example, there is the possibility that there is such a thing as winter. For the Ojibwa, winter is personified by Keewatin, spirit of the north. And then of course there is the possibility that the male being is not sufficient unto himself. Why else the need for women? It was this feminine potential, personified as the spirit Geezhigo-Quae, to whom Kitchi Manitou ascended. I say ascended because Geezhigo-Quae (Sky Woman) lived on the Moon. Kitchi Manitou, the greatest of spirits, the most powerful being in the universe had to ask a woman for help. He asked if she would bear his essence. He asked if she would join with him in creating an image of himself in the world. He asked if she would love and nurture his children. Sky Woman agreed. They joined together and Sky Woman became pregnant with the children of Kitchi Manitou. And then the blighter disappeared. He went off and did whatever men and Manitou's do after they get their women pregnant! So, Sky Woman went down to Mother Earth to prepare for the birth herself. She bent trees for a lodge. Tanned hides to cover it. Dried meat for the winter. Many animals passed by to ask what she was up to. She explained that she was carrying Manitou's children and was preparing a home for them. The word spread across the world. Most creatures were happy and excited that Manitou had given them the gift of his children.

Every life form that lived on Mother Earth needed water. The supply of water was controlled by the Water Manitous. They knew that Kitchi Manitou was the most powerful of spirits and if his children walked the Earth their powers over the water would be diminished. Actually, the Water Manitous weren't just mad. They were enraged! In retaliation they used their powers to cause a great flood that spread across the entire world. As the waters rose and destroyed her encampment Sky Woman retreated to the Moon. She looked down in dismay. Water covered the land, her man was gone who knows where, and she - pregnant with his children -was left to handle the chaos by herself.

But like every woman, Geezhigo-Quae had a mind of her own. She wasn't helpless. She knew that she could influence her own destiny. She could have a say in how things turned out. She made a plan.

Although the world was inundated with water below her, Sky Woman could see a few animals that were not under the total control of the Water Spirits. That was because although they breathed air, they knew how to swim!

The first creature she called to her aid was the giant turtle. But she asked other creatures to help her, too. The loon, the beaver, even the little muskrat were among her assistants that day.

"I don't have all the powers of creation that Kitchi Manitou has. But I'm a woman and I have a special gift. I have the power to re-create. I can re-create Manitou's world, but I can't do it by myself. I need your help. I need you to dive deep. I need you to dive deep enough that you can bring me a handful of the original soil made by Manitou. The soil will be the seed I use to re-create the Earth."

The giant sea turtle went first because he was the biggest. He tried and tried but couldn't descend to the bottom of the rising waters. When he came to the surface for the last time, he invited Geeshigo-Quae to come down from the Moon and sit on his back so that she could direct the operations. All afternoon the loon and the beaver took turns diving, but they just couldn't get to the bottom of the murky depths. At the end of the day, it was only the little muskrat who hadn't given it a try. Not because he didn't want to help, but because everyone knew that muskrats don't really dive deep.

Muskrats live in shallow sloughs, or at the edge of rivers and lakes. You'll never see them swimming in the deepest water. But if you look at your own life, you'll see that there are times when you just have to give up your old story about what you can or cannot do. Sometimes in your life you have to burst from the confines of your story and grow into a more capable person. That day, long ago, the muskrat decided that with no one else available to help it was up to him to do the job. He took a deep breath. Then another. And another. Then in an instant he disappeared below the surface.

They waited and waited...but the muskrat didn't return. The sun dipped below the horizon. They waited. The moon cast a sad blue glow across the water. They waited. It was a long night.

As the sky grew light Geezhigo-Quae scanned the waves. She strained to catch sight of the muskrat. Suddenly she gasped. She pointed across the water. Something floated in the distance. The turtle swam quickly towards it and as they got close Sky Woman realized it was the muskrat...but he was dead.

She pulled him from the water, sad that he'd given his life trying to help her build a home for her children. She cradled him in her arms and saw that one of his paws was clutched tightly. Gently she pried it open. There was the soil from Manitou's world! The little muskrat did it! He did what the bigger animals couldn't. He did what no other muskrat had done before. Geezhigo-Quae was so happy. Now she could create a home for Manitou's children! To thank the muskrat, she bent over and breathed life back into him . . . which is why we still have muskrats today.

Then she took the soil and breathed into it the characteristics that would allow it to provide nourishment, shelter, teachings and incentive to the beings that would live upon it. That soil she rubbed on the turtle's back. She rubbed the soil round and round. As she did so the Muzzu-kummick-quae again took shape above the water. Geezhigo-Quae continued to move over the new soil. She walked in wider and wider circles. And the Earth was re-created.

Forever after the Ojibwa called this land Turtle Island. Eventually Kitchi Manitou returned and was grateful to Geezhigo-Quae for her strength and her compassion. He decided that she must have a new name --- a name that would always be voiced with honor and respect. Thereafter she was known as Nokomis --- the Great Mother, creator of the Anishinabeg, the Good Beings.

The children of Kitchi Manitou and Nokomis had children...and the children had children. As time went on and people spread across the land, they sometimes called themselves Ojibwa, sometimes Chippewa, or Ottawa, Pottawatomi and Mississauga. Eventually they were known as Canadians and Americans.

GREAT SERPENT AND THE GREAT FLOOD

One day when Nanabozho returned to his lodge after a long journey, he missed his young cousin who lived with him. He called the cousin's name but heard no answer. Looking around on the sand for tracks, Nanabozho was startled by the trail of the Great Serpent. He then knew that his cousin had been seized by his enemy.

Nanabozho picked up his bow and arrows and followed the track of the serpent. He passed the great river, climbed mountains, and crossed over valleys until he came to the shores of a deep and gloomy lake. It is now called Manitou Lake, Spirit Lake, and also the Lake of Devils. The trail of the Great Serpent led to the edge of the water.

Nanabozho could see at the bottom of the lake, the house of the Great Serpent. It was filled with evil spirits, who were his servants and his companions. Their forms were monstrous and terrible. Most of them, like their master, resembled spirits. In the center of this horrible group was the Great Serpent himself, coiling his terrifying length around the cousin of Nanabozho.

The head of the Serpent was red as blood. His fierce eyes glowed like fire. His entire body was armed with hard and glistening scales of every color and shade.

Looking down on these twisting spirits of evil, Nanabozho made up his mind that he would get revenge on them for the death of his cousin.

He said to the clouds, "Disappear!"

And the clouds went out of sight.

"Winds, be still at once!" And the winds became still.

When the air over the lake of evil spirits had become stagnant, Nanabozho said to the sun, "Shine over the lake with all the fierceness you can. Make the water boil."

In these ways, thought Nanabozho, he would force the Great Serpent to seek the cool shade of the trees growing on the shores of the lake. There he would seize the enemy and get revenge.

After giving his orders, Nanabozho took his bow and arrows and placed himself near the spot where he thought the serpents would come to enjoy the shade. Then he changed himself into the broken stump of a withered tree.

The winds became still, the air stagnant, and the sun shot hot rays from a cloudless sky. In time, the water of the lake became troubled, and bubbles rose to the surface. The rays of the sun had penetrated to the home of the serpents. As the water bubbled and foamed, a serpent lifted his head above the center of the lake and gazed around the shores. Soon another serpent came to the surface. Both listened for the footsteps of Nanabozho, but they heard him nowhere.

"Nanabozho is sleeping," they said to one another.

And then they plunged beneath the waters, which seemed to hiss as they closed over the evil spirits.

Not long after, the lake became more troubled. Its water boiled from its very depths, and the hot waves dashed wildly against the rocks on its banks. Soon the

Great Serpent came slowly to the surface of the water and moved toward the shore. His blood-red crest glowed. The reflection from his scales was blinding--as blinding as the glitter of a sleet-covered forest beneath the winter sun. He was followed by all the evil spirits. So great was their number that they soon covered the shores of the lake.

When they saw the broken stump of the withered tree, they suspected that it might be one of the disguises of Nanabozho. They knew his cunning. One of the serpents approached the stump, wound his tail around it, and tried to drag it down into the lake. Nanabozho could hardly keep from crying aloud, for the tail of the monster prickled his sides. But he stood firm and was silent.

The evil spirits moved on. The Great Serpent glided into the forest and wound his many coils around the trees. His companions also found shade--all but one. One remained near the shore to listen for the footsteps of Nanabozho.

From the stump, Nanabozho watched until all the serpents were asleep, and the guard was intently looking in another direction. Then he silently drew an arrow from his quiver, placed it in his bow, and aimed it at the heart of the Great Serpent. It reached its mark. With a howl that shook the mountains and startled the wild beasts in their caves, the monster awoke. Followed by its terrified companions, which also were howling with rage and terror, the Great Serpent plunged into the water.

At the bottom of the lake there still lay the body of Nanabozho's cousin. In their fury the serpents tore it into a thousand pieces. His shredded lungs rose to the surface and covered the lake with whiteness.

The Great Serpent soon knew that he would die from his wound, but he and his companions were determined to destroy Nanabozho. They caused the water of the lake to swell upward and to pound against the shore with the sound of many thunders. Madly the flood rolled over the land, over the tracks of Nanabozho, carrying with it rocks and trees. High on the crest of the highest wave floated the wounded Great Serpent. His eyes glared around him, and his hot breath mingled with the hot breath of his many companions.

Nanabozho, fleeing before the angry waters, thought of his Indian children. He ran through their villages, shouting, "Run to the mountaintops! The Great Serpent is angry and is flooding the earth! Run! Run!"

The people caught up their children and found safety on the mountains. Nanabozho continued his flight along the base of the western hills and then up a high mountain beyond Lake Superior, far to the north. There he found many men and animals that had escaped from the flood that was already covering the valleys and plains and even the highest hills. Still the waters continued to rise. Soon all the mountains were under the flood, except the high one on which stood Nanabozho.

There he gathered together timber and made a raft. Upon it the men and women and animals with him placed themselves. Almost immediately the mountaintop disappeared from their view, and they floated along on the face of the waters. For many days they floated. At long last, the flood began to subside. Soon the people on the raft saw the trees on the tops of the mountains. Then they saw the mountains and hills, then the plains and the valleys.

When the water disappeared from the land, the people who survived learned that the Great Serpent was dead and that his companions had returned to the bottom of the lake of spirits. There they remain to this day. For fear of Nanabozho, they have never dared to come forth again.

HOW DOGS CAME TO THE INDIANS

Two Ojibwa Indians in a canoe had been blown far from shore by a great wind. They had gone far and were hungry and lost. They had little strength left to paddle, so they drifted before the wind. At last, their canoe was blown onto a beach, and they were glad, but not for long. Looking for the tracks of animals, they saw some huge footprints which they knew must be those of a giant. They were afraid and hid in the bushes. As they crouched low, a big arrow thudded into the ground close beside them. Then a huge giant came toward them. A caribou hung from his belt, but the man was so big that it looked like a rabbit. He told them that he did not hurt people and he like to be a friend to little people, who seemed to the giant to be so helpless.

He asked the two lost Indians to come home with him, and since they had no food and their weapons had been lost in the storm at sea, they were glad to go with him. An evil Windigo spirit came to the lodge of the giant and told the two men that the giant had other men hidden away in the forest because he like to eat them. The Windigo pretended to be a friend, but he was the one who wanted the men because he was an eater of people. The Windigo became very angry when the giant would not give him the two men, and finally the giant became angry too. He took a big stick and turned over a big bowl with it. A strange animal which the Indians had never seen before lay on the floor, looking up at them. It looked like a wolf to them, but the giant called the animal 'Dog.' The giant told him to kill the evil Windigo spirit. The beast sprang to its feet, shook himself, and started to grow, and grow, and grow. The more he shook himself, the more he grew and the fiercer he became. He sprang at the Windigo and killed him; then the dog grew smaller and smaller and crept under the bowl.

The giant saw that the Indians were much surprised and pleased with Dog and said that he would give it to them, though it was his pet. He told the men that he would command Dog to take them home. They had no idea how this could be done, though they had seen that the giant was a maker of magic, but they thanked the friendly giant for his great gift. The giant took the men and the dog to the seashore and gave the dog a command. At once it began to grow bigger and bigger, until it was nearly as big as a horse. The giant put the two men onto the back of the dog and told them to hold on very tightly. As Dog ran into the sea, he grew still bigger and when the water was deep enough, he started to swim strongly away from the shore.

After a very long time, the two Ojibwa began to see a part of the seacoast which they knew, and soon the dog headed for shore. As he neared the beach, he became smaller and smaller so that the Indians had to swim for the last part of their journey. The dog left them close to their lodges and disappeared into the forest. When the men told their tribe of their adventure, the people though that the men were speaking falsely. "Show us even the little mystery animal, Dog, and we shall believe you," a chief said.

A few moons came and went and then, one morning while the tribe slept, the dog returned to the two men. It allowed them to pet it and took food from their hands. The tribe was very much surprised to see this new creature. It stayed with the tribe.

That, as the Indians tell, was how the first dog came to the earth.

Plains Ojibwe man, southern Manitoba

THE ORIGIN OF THE BIG DIPPER

Fisher was a great hunter. He was not big, but he was known for his determination and was regarded as one with great power. Fisher's son wanted to be a great hunter also. One day the son went out to try to catch something. It was not easy, for the snow was very deep and it was very cold everywhere. In those days it was always winter on the Earth and there was no such thing as warm weather. The son hunted a long time with no luck. Finally, though, he saw a squirrel. As quietly as he could he sneaked up and then pounced, catching the squirrel between his paws. Before he could kill it, though, the squirrel spoke to him. "Grandson," said the squirrel, "don't kill me. I can give you some good advice."

"Speak then," said the young fisher.

"I see that you are shivering from the cold. If you do what I tell you, we may all enjoy warm weather. Then it will be easy for all of us to find food and not starve as we are doing now."

"Tell me what to do, Grandfather," the young fisher said, letting the squirrel go.

The squirrel climbed quickly up onto a high branch and then spoke again. "Go home and say nothing. Just sit down in your lodge and begin to weep. Your mother will ask you what is wrong, but you must not answer her. If she tries to comfort you or give you food, you must refuse it. When your father comes home, he will ask you why you are weeping. Then you can speak. Tell him the winds are too cold and the snow is too deep. Tell him that he must bring warm weather to the Earth."

So, the young fisher went home. He sat in the corner of the lodge and cried. His mother asked what was wrong, but he did not answer. She offered him food, but he pushed it away. When his father returned and saw his only son weeping, he went to his side.

" What is wrong, son?" Fisher said.

Then the young fisher said what the squirrel had told him to say. " I am weeping because the wind is too cold, and the snow is too deep. We are all starving because of the winter. I want you to use your powers to bring the warm weather."

"The thing you are asking of me is hard to do," said Fisher, "but you are right. I will do all I can to grant your wish. "Then Fisher had a great feast. He invited all of his friends and told them what he planned to do. "I am going to the place where the skyland is closest to the Earth," he said. "There in the skyland the people have all the warm weather. I intend to go there to bring some of that warm weather back. Then snow will go away, and we will have plenty to eat."

All of Fisher's friends were pleased and offered to go with him. So, when Fisher set out, he took the strongest of his friends along. Those friends were Otter, Lynx and Wolverine. The four of them traveled for a long time through the snow. They went toward the mountains, higher and higher each day. Fisher had with him a pack filled with dried venison and they slept at night buried under the snow. At last, after many, many days, they came to the highest mountain and climbed to its top. Then Fisher took a pipe and tobacco out of his pouch.

"We must offer our smoke to the Four Directions," Fisher said. The four of them smoked and sent their prayers to Gitchee Manitou, asking for success.

The sky was very close above them, but they had to find some way to break through into the land above. "We must jump up," said Fisher. "Who will go first?"

"I will try," said Otter. He leaped up and struck the sky but did not break through. Instead, he fell back and slid on his belly all the way to the bottom of the mountain. To this day all otters slide like that in the snow.

"Now it is my turn," said Lynx. He jumped too, striking hard against the sky and falling back unconscious. Fisher tried then, but even he did not have enough power.

"Now it is your turn," said Fisher to Wolverine. "You are the strongest of us all."

Wolverine leaped. He struck hard against the sky and fell back, but he did not give up. He leaped again and again until he had made a crack in the sky. Once more he leaped and finally broke through. Fisher jumped through the hole in the sky after him.

The skyland was a beautiful place. It was warm and sunny, and there were plants and flowers of all kinds growing. They could hear the singing of birds all around them, but they could see no people. They went farther and found many long lodges. When they looked inside, they found that there were cages in the lodges. Each cage held a different bird.

"These will make for fine hunting," Fisher said. "Let us set them free."

Quickly Wolverine and Fisher chewed through the rawhide that bound the cages together and freed the birds. The birds all flew down through the hole in the sky. so, there are many kinds of birds in the world today.

Wolverine and Fisher now began to make the hole in the skyland bigger. The warmth of the skyland began to fall through the hole and the land below began to grow warmer. The snow began to melt and the grass and plants beneath the snow began to turn green.

But the sky people came out when they saw what was happening. They ran toward Wolverine and Fisher, shouting loudly. "Thieves," they shouted. "Stop taking our warm weather!"

Wolverine jumped back through the hole to escape, but Fisher kept making the hole bigger. He knew that if he didn't make it big enough, the sky people would quickly close the hole again and it would be winter again in the land below. He chewed the hole larger and larger. Finally, just when the sky people were very close, he stopped. The hole was big enough for enough warm weather for half of the year to escape through, but it was not big enough for enough warm weather to last all the time. That is why the winter still comes back every year. Fisher knew that the sky people might try to close the hole in the sky. He had to take their attention away from it and so he taunted them.

"I am Fisher, the great hunter," he said. "You cannot catch me." Then he ran to the tallest tree in the skyland. All the sky people ran after him. Just as they were about to grab him, he leaped up into the tree and climbed to the highest branches, where no one could follow. At first the sky people did not know what to do. Then they began to shoot arrows at him. But Fisher wasn't hurt, for he had a special power. There was only one place on his tail where an arrow could kill him.

Finally, though, the sky people guessed where his magic was and shot at that place. An arrow struck the fatal spot. Fisher turned over on his back and began to fall.

But Fisher never struck the Earth. Gitchee Manitou took pity on him because he had kept his promise and done something to help all the people. Gitchee Manitou placed Fisher high up in the sky among the stars.

If you look up into the sky, you can still see him, even though some people call that pattern of stars The Big Dipper. Every year he crosses the sky. When the arrow strikes him, he rolls over onto his back in the winter sky. But when the winter is almost ended, he faithfully turns to his feet and starts out once more on his long journey to bring the warm weather back to the Earth.

THEFT OF FIRE

Once, many years ago, Manabozho asked his grandmother, Nolomis, why the people had to freeze all winter long, in the cold, northern weather. He wanted to know if there was not some way in which the people could manage to stay warm and cozy, through the long winters.

Nokomis answered that it was rumored that, in a far-off land, an old man had the gift of fire. However, he was a selfish person, and refused to give it to anyone else. Instead, he kept it hidden, to be used only by himself and his daughters.

Manabozho told Nokomis that he wanted to journey to this land, in order, to get some of this fire, from the old man. Nokomis didn't want Manabozho to travel so far, but she knew that he would go anyone, once his mind was set. So, she wished him well, as he set off. As Manabozho left their camp, he told his grandmother to be ready with the kindling, when he returned.

When Manabozho came close, to the camp, of the old man, he decided to stop and think of a plan for getting inside. He decided to disguise himself as a rabbit, hoping that the man's daughters would feel sorry for him and carry him inside, away from the cold.

Manabozho's plan worked just as he had expected and the younger daughter, seeing him shivering in the cold, tucked him under her shawl, and carried him inside.

The old man, however, was very angry about this. He did not allow any strange beings in his lodge, not even a rabbit. Growing drowsy from the fire's warmth, however, the old man fell asleep and didn't think of the rabbit again.

The girls put the rabbit (Now, remember, this was really Manabozho) near the fire to warm and left him to prepare their father's dinner. No sooner had the girls turned their backs, than Manabozho caught a spark of fire, on his back, and ran off. When the girls realized that they had been fooled, there was quite a commotion, but by then, there was nothing that they could do about it.

Manabozho ran and ran. As he neared the camp, he called out to Nokomis to have the kindling ready. Of course, she did. She took the spark of fire from the rabbit's back, and soon had the fire burning, in their lodge.

By now, Manabozho had changed back into himself, and he went outside and called, to the people, to come and take a spark, from the fire. He told them that in that manner, they would be able to keep themselves, and their children warm, throughout the long, cold winter months.

TREATY

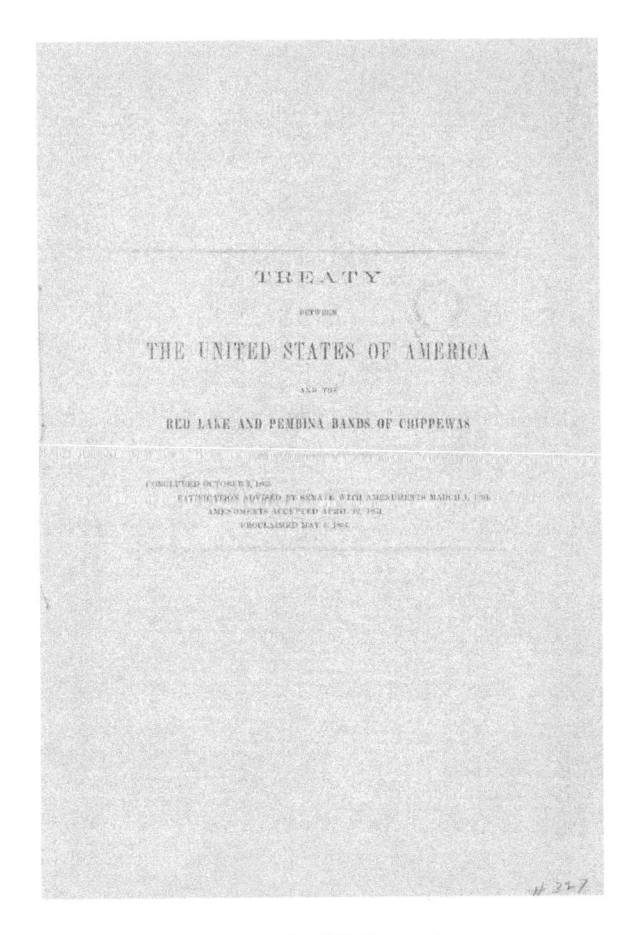

BETWEEN

THE UNITED STATES OF AMERICA

AND THE

RED LAKE AND PEMBINA BANDS OF CHIPPEWAS

Treaty of Old Crossing

THE DREAM FAST

Long ago, as it still is today, it was the custom for a boy who reached a certain age to go into the forest and wait for a dream. He would build a small lodge and go without food for many days in the hope he would be visited by some animal or spirit of the forest that would take pity on him and give guidance and power.

There was a boy named Opichi who reached that age. Opichi's father was very respected in the village, and he was determined that his son would be given a dream of such power that no one else could compare with him. So eager was the father for his son to get power that he insisted the boy go on his dream fast before the last snow left the ground, even though most boys would wait until the time when the ground was warm, and the leaves returned to the trees.

"My son is strong," said the father. "He will go now. He will gain greater strength from the cold."

Opichi was a boy who always wished to please his parents and so he did as his father said. They went together into the forest and the father selected a spot-on top of a small hill. There Opichi made a small lean-to of saplings, covering it with hemlock boughs. He sat beneath it on the bare ground with a thin piece of deerskin wrapped about his shoulders.

"I will return each day at dawn," the father said. "You will tell me then what you have seen."

That night the north wind, the icy breath of the Great Bear, blew cold. Opichi's mother was concerned, but the father did not worry. "My son is strong," he said. "This cold wind will make his vision a better one."

When the morning came, he went to the lean-to and shook the poles. "My son," he said, "tell me what you have seen."

Opichi crawled out and looked up at his father. "Father," the boy said, "a deer came to the lodge and spoke to me."

"That is good." said the father. "But you must continue to fast. Surely a greater vision will come to you."

"I will continue to watch and wait," Opichi said.

Opichi's father left his son and went back to his lodge. That night a light snow fell. "I'm worried about our son," said Opichi's mother.

"Do not worry," said the father. "The snow will only make whatever dream comes to him more powerful."

When morning came, the father went into the forest again, climbed the hill and shook the poles, calling his son out.

"Father," Opichi said as he emerged, shaking from the cold, "last night a beaver came to me. It taught me a song."

"That is good," said the father. "You are doing well. You will gain even more power if you stay longer."

"I will watch and wait," said the boy.

So, it went for four more days. Each morning his father asked Opichi what he had seen. Each time the boy told of his experiences from the night before. Now hawk and wolf, bear and eagle had visited the boy. Each day Opichi looked thinner and weaker, but he agreed to stay and wait for an ever-greater vision to please his father.

At last, on the morning of the seventh day, Opichi's mother spoke to her husband. "Our son has waited long enough in the forest. I will go with you this morning and we will bring him home."

Opichi's mother and father went together into the forest. The gentle breath of the Fawn, the warm south wind of spring, had blown during the night and all the snow had melted away. As they climbed the hill, they heard a birdsong coming from above them. It was a song they had never heard before. It sounded almost like the name of their son. Opi chi chi. Opi chi chi.

When they reached the lodge, Opichi's father shook the poles. "My son," he said, "it is time to end your fast. It is time to come home."

There was no answer. Opichi's mother and father bent down to look into the small lean-to of hemlock boughs and saplings. As they did so, a bird came flying out. It was gray and black with a red chest. Opi chi chi. Opi chi chi.

So, it sang as it perched on a branch above them. Then it spoke.

"My parents," said the bird, "you see me as I am now. The one who was your son is gone. You sent him out too early and asked him to wait for power too long. Now I will return each spring when the gentle breath of the Fawn comes to our land. My song will let people know it is the time for a boy to go on his dream fast. But your words must help to remind his parents not to make their son stay out too long."

Then, singing that song, which was the name of their son, the robin flew off into the forest.

1944	2009	G-450	Hamley, Leonard	husb	1883	M
1945	2010	GF-17	" Josephine	wife	1891	F
1946	2011		" Peter Leonard	son	1917	M
1947	2012		" Rosalie Stella	dtr	1919	F
1948	2013		" Celia	dtr	1921	F
1949	2014		" Bernard	son	1922	M
1950	2015		" Leo Sylvester	son	1924	M
1951	2016		" Joseph Frederick	son	1926	M
1952	2017		" Clearance Patrick	son	1928	M
1953	2018	GF-151	* Hamley, Patrick	husb	1887	M
1954	----	Not enrolled	" Mazie	wife	----	F
1954	2019		" Ellens Joyce	dtr	1917	F
1955	2020	G-449	Harris, Rebecca	wife	1885	F
----	----	Not enrolled	" Paul	husb		M
1956	2021	G-011394	" Louella Elizabeth	dtr	1909	F
1957	2022		" Leonard P.	son	1911	M
1958	2023		" Clemence	dtr	1914	F
1959	2024		" Eleanor	dtr	1915	F
1960	2025	G-384 Shakipishkwa	Hayder, Mrs. Alex	wife	1879	F
----	----	Not enrolled	" Alexander	husb	1887	M
1961	2026		" Joseph	son	1909	M

Indian census rolls, 1885-1940

MANABOZHO'S ADVENTURES

Manabozho saw a number of ducks, and he thought to himself, "Just how am I going to kill them?" After a while, he took out one of his pails and started to drum and sing at the same time. The words of the song he sang were: "I am bringing new songs."

When the ducks saw Manabozho standing near the shore, they swam toward him and as soon as he saw this, he sent his grandmother ahead to build a little lodge, where they could live. In the meantime, he killed a few of the ducks, so, while his grandmother started out to build a shelter, Manabozho went towards the lake where the ducks and geese were floating around and around. Manabozho jumped into a sack and then dived into the water. The ducks and geese were quite surprised to see that he was such an excellent diver and came closer and closer. Then Manabozho challenged them to a contest at diving. He said that he could beat them all. The ducks all accepted the challenge, but Manabozho beat them. Then he went after the geese and beat them too. For a time, he was alternately diving and rising to the surface, all around. Finally, he dived under the geese and started to tie their legs together with some basswood bark. When the geese noticed this, they tried to rise and fly away, but they were unable to do so, for Manabozho was hanging on to the other end of the string. The geese, nevertheless, managed to rise, gradually dragging Manabozho along with them. They finally emerged from the water and rose higher and higher into the air. Manabozho, however, hung on, and would not let go, until his hand was cut and the string broke.

While walking along the river he saw some berries in the water. He dived down for them but was stunned when he unexpectedly struck the bottom. There he lay for quite a while, and when he recovered consciousness and looked up, he saw the berries hanging on a tree just above him.

While Manabozho was once walking along a lake shore, tired and hungry, he observed a long, narrow sandbar, which extended far out into the water, around which were myriads of waterfowl, so Manabozho decided to have a feast. He had with him only his medicine bag; so he entered the brush and hung it upon a tree, now called "Manabozho tree," and procured a quantity of bark, which he rolled into a bundle and placing it upon his back, returned to the shore, where he pretended to pass slowly by in sight of the birds. Some of the Swans and Ducks, however, recognizing Manabozho and becoming frightened, moved away from the shore.

One of the Swans called out, "Ho! Manabozho, where are you going?" To this Manabozho replied, "I am going to have a song. As you may see, I have all my songs with me." Manabozho then called out to the birds, "Come to me, my brothers, and let us sing and dance." The birds assented and returned to the shore, when all retreated a short distance away from the lake to an open space where they might dance. Manabozho removed the bundle of bark from his back and placed it on the ground, got out his singing-sticks, and said to the birds, "Now, all of you dance around me as I drum; sing as loudly as you can, and keep your eyes closed. The first one to open his eyes will forever have them red and sore."

Manabozho began to beat time upon his bundle of bark, while the birds, with eyes closed, circled around him singing as loudly as they could. Keeping time with one hand, Manabozho suddenly grasped the neck of a Swan, which he broke; but before he had killed the bird it screamed out, whereupon Manabozho said, "That's right, brothers, sing as loudly as you can." Soon another Swan fell a victim; then a Goose, and so on until the number of birds was greatly reduced. Then the "Helldiver," opening his eyes to see why there was less singing than at first, and beholding Manabozho and the heap of victims, cried out, "Manabozho is killing us! Manabozho is killing us!" and immediately ran to the water, followed by the remainder of the birds.

As the "Helldiver" was a poor runner, Manabozho soon overtook him, and said, "I won't kill you, but you shall always have red eyes and be the laughingstock of all the birds." With this he gave the bird a kick, sending him far out into the lake and knocking off his tail, so that the "Helldiver" is red-eyed and tailless to this day.

Manabozho then gathered up his birds and taking them out upon the sandbar buried them--some with their heads protruding others with the feet sticking out of the sand. He then built a fire to cook the game, but as this would require some time, and as Manabozho was tired after his exertion, he stretched himself on the ground to sleep. In order to be informed if anyone approached, he slapped his thigh and said to it "You watch the birds and awaken me if anyone should come near them." Then, with his back to the fire, he fell asleep.

After a while a party of Indians came along in their canoes, and seeing the feast in store, went to the sandbar and pulled out every bird which Manabozho had so carefully placed there, but put back the heads and feet in such a way that there was no indication that the bodies had been disturbed. When the Indians had finished eating, they departed, taking with them all the food that remained from the feast.

Sometime afterward, Manabozho awoke, and being very hungry, bethought himself to enjoy the fruits of his stratagem. In attempting to pull a baked swan from the sand he found nothing but the head and neck, which he held in his hand. Then he tried another and found the body of that bird also gone. So, he tried another, and then another, but each time met with disappointment. Who could have robbed him? he thought. He struck his thigh and asked, "Who has been here to rob me of my feast; did I not command you to watch while I slept?" His thigh responded, "I also fell asleep, as I was very tired; but I see some people moving rapidly away in their canoes; perhaps they were the thieves. I see also they are very dirty and poorly dressed." Then Manabozho ran out to the point of the sandbar, and beheld the people in their canoes, just disappearing around a point of land. Then he called to them and reviled them, calling them "Winnibe'go! Winnibe'go! " And by this term the Menomini have ever since designated their thievish neighbors.

After this Manabozho began travelling again. One time he feasted a lot of animals. He had killed a big bear, which was very fat, and he began cooking it, having made a fire with his bow-drill. When he was ready to spread his meat, he heard two trees scraping together, swayed by the wind. He didn't like this noise while he was having his feast and he thought he could stop it. He climbed up one of the trees and when he reached the spot where the two trees were scraping, his foot got caught in a crack between the trees and he could not free himself.

When the first animal guest came along and saw Manabozho in the tree, he, the Beaver, said "Come on to the feast, Manabozho is caught and can't stop us." And then the other animals came. The Beaver jumped into the grease and ate it, and the Otter did the same, and that is why they are so fat in the belly. The Beaver scooped up the grease and smeared it on himself, and that is the reason why he is so fat now. All the small animals came and got fat for themselves. Last of all the animals came the Rabbit, when nearly all the grease was gone - only a little left. So, he put some on the nape of his neck and some on his groin and for this reason he has only a little fat in those places. So, all the animals got their fat except Rabbit. Then they all went, and poor Manabozho got free at last. He looked around and found a bear's skull that was all cleaned except for the brain, and there was only a little of that left, but he couldn't get at it. Then he wished himself to be changed into an ant in order to get into the skull and get enough to eat, for there was only about an ant's meal left.

Then he became an ant and entered the skull. When he had enough, he turned back into a man, but he had his head inside the skull; this allowed him to walk but not to see.[86] On account of this he had no idea where he was. Then he felt the trees. He said to one, "What are you?" It answered, "Cedar." He kept doing this with all the trees in order to keep his course. When he got too near the shore, he knew it by the kind of trees he met. So, he kept on walking and the only tree that did not answer promptly was the black spruce, and that said "I'm Se'segandak" (black spruce). Then Manabozho knew he was on low ground. He came to a lake, but he did not know how large it was, as he couldn't see. He started to swim across. An Ojibwa was paddling on the lake with his family, and he heard someone calling, "Hey! There's a bear swimming across the lake." Manabozho became frightened at this, and the Ojibwa then said, "He's getting near the shore now." So Manabozho swam faster, and as he could understand the Ojibwa language, he guided himself by the cries. He landed on a smooth rock, slipped and broke the bear's skull, which fell off his head. Then the Ojibwa cried out, "That's no bear! That's Manabozho!" Manabozho was all right, now that he could see, so he ran off, as he didn't want to stay with these people.

Kakenwash

MANABOZHO AND THE MAPLE TREES

A very long time ago, when the world was new, Gitchee Manitou made things so that life was very easy for the people. There was plenty of game and the weather was always good and the maple trees were filled with thick sweet syrup. Whenever anyone wanted to get maple syrup from the trees, all they had to do was break off a twig and collect it as it dripped out.

One day, Manabozho went walking around. "I think I'll go see how my friends the Anishinabe are doing," he said. So, he went to a village of Indian people. But there was no one around. So, Manbozho looked for the people. They were not fishing in the streams or the lake. They were not working in the fields hoeing their crops. They were not gathering berries. Finally, he found them. They were in the grove of maple trees near the village. They were just lying on their backs with their mouths open, letting maple syrup drip into their mouths.

"This will NOT do!" Manabozho said. "My people are all going to be fat and lazy if they keep on living this way."

So, Manabozho went down to the river. He took with him a big basket he had made of birch bark. With this basket, he brought back many buckets of water. He went to the top of the maple trees and poured water in, so that it thinned out the syrup. Now, thick maple syrup no longer dripped out of the broken twigs. Now what came out was thin and watery and just barely sweet to the taste.

"This is how it will be from now on," Manabozho said. "No longer will syrup drip from the maple trees. Now there will only be this watery sap. When people want to make maple syrup, they will have to gather many buckets full of the sap in a birch bark basket like mine. They will have to gather wood and make fires so they can heat stones to drop into the baskets. They will have to boil the water with the heated stones for a long time to make even a little maple syrup. Then my people will no longer grow fat and lazy. Then they will appreciate this maple syrup Gitchee Manitou made available to them. Not only that, but this sap will also drip only from the trees at a certain time of the year. Then it will not keep people from hunting and fishing and gathering and hoeing in the fields. This is how it is going to be," Manabozho said.

And that is how it is to this day.

Misko-Benais - Red Thunder

THE GIRLS WHO WISHED TO MARRY STARS

In the wintertime they used birch bark wigwams. All the animals could then. talk together. Two girls, who were very foolish, talked foolishly and were in no respect like the other girls of their tribe, made their bed out-of-doors, and slept right out under the stars. The very fact that they slept outside during the winter proves how foolish they were.

One of these girls asked the other, "With what star would you like to sleep, the white one or the red one?" The other girl answered, "I'd like to sleep with the red star." "Oh, that's all right," said the first one, "I would like to sleep with the white star. He's the younger; the red is the older." Then the two girls fell asleep. When they awoke, they found themselves in another world, the star world. There were four of them there, the two girls and the two stars who had become men. The white star was very, very old and was gray-headed, while the younger was red-headed. He was the red star. The girls stayed a long time in this star world, and the one who had chosen the white star was very sorry, for he was so old.

There was an old woman up in this world who sat over a hole in the sky, and, whenever she moved, she showed them the hole and said, "That's where you came from." They looked down through and saw their people playing down below, and then the girls grew very sorry and very homesick. One evening, near sunset, the old woman moved a little way from the hole.

The younger girl heard the noise of the mitewin down below. When it was almost daylight, the old woman sat over the hole again and the noise of mitewin stopped; it was her spirit that made the noise. She was the guardian of the mitewin.

One morning the old woman told the girls, "If you want to go down where you came from, we will let you down, but get to work and gather roots to make a string-made rope, twisted. The two of you make coils of rope as high as your heads when you are sitting. Two coils will be enough." The girls worked for days until they had accomplished this. They made plenty of rope and tied it to a big basket. They then got into the basket and the people of the star world lowered them down. They descended right into an Eagle's nest, but the people above thought the girls were on the ground and stopped lowering them. They were obliged to stay in the nest, because they could do nothing to help themselves.

Said one, "We'll have to stay here until someone comes to get us." Bear passed by. The girls cried out, "Bear, come and get us. You are going to get married sometime. Now is your chance!" Bear thought, "They are not very good-looking women." He pretended to climb up and then said, "I can't climb up any further." And he went away, for the girls didn't suit him. Next came Lynx. The girls cried out again, "Lynx, come up and get us. You will go after women some day!" Lynx answered, "I can't, for I have no claws," and he went away. Then an ugly-looking man, Wolverine, passed and the girls spoke to him. "Hey, wolverine, come and get us." Wolverine started to climb up, for he thought it a very fortunate thing to have these women and was very glad. When he reached them, they placed their hair ribbons in the nest. Then Wolverine agreed to take one girl at a time, so he took the first one down and went back for the next. Then Wolverine went away with his two wives and enjoyed himself greatly, as he was ugly and nobody else would have him. They went far into the woods, and then they sat down and began to talk. "Oh!" cried one of the girls, "I forgot my hair ribbon." Then Wolverine said, "I will run back for it." And he started off to get the hair ribbons. Then the girls hid and told the trees, whenever Wolverine should come back and whistle for them, to answer him by whistling. Wolverine soon returned and began to whistle for his wives, and the trees all around him whistled in answer. Wolverine, realizing that he had been tricked, gave up the search and departed very angry.

WENEBOJO AND THE WOLVES

One day Wenebojo saw some people and went up to see who they were. He was surprised to find that they were a pack of wolves. He called them nephews and asked what they were doing. They were hunting, said the Old Wolf, and looking for a place to camp. So, they all camped together on the edge of a lake.

Wenebojo was very cold for there were only two logs for the fire, so one of the wolves jumped over the fire and immediately it burned higher. Wenebojo was hungry, so one of the wolves pulled off his moccasin and tossed it to Wenebojo and told him to pull out the sock. Wenebojo threw it back, saying that he didn't eat any stinking socks. The wolf said: "You must be very particular if you don't like this food."

He reached into the sock and pulled out a deer tenderloin then reached in again and brought out some bear fat. Wenebojo's eyes popped. He asked for some of the meat and started to roast it over the fire. Then, imitating the wolf, Wenebojo pulled off his moccasin and threw it at the wolf, saying, "Here, nephew, you must be hungry. Pull my sock out." But there was no sock, only old dry hay that he used to keep his feet warm. The wolf said he didn't eat hay and Wenebojo was ashamed.

The next day the wolves left to go hunting, but the father of the young wolves came along with Wenebojo. As they traveled along, they found an old deer carcass. Old Wolf told Wenebojo to pick it up, but Wenebojo said he didn't want it and kicked it aside. The Wolf picked it up and shook it: it was a nice, tanned deerskin which Wenebojo wanted, so Old Wolf gave it to him. They went on, following the wolves. Wenebojo saw blood and soon they came on the pack, all lying asleep with their bellies full; only the bones were left. Wenebojo was mad because the young wolves were so greedy and had eaten up all the deer. The Old Wolf then woke up the others and told them to pack the deer home. Wenebojo picked up the best bones so he could boil them. When they reached camp, the fire was still burning, and Old Wolf told the others to give Wenebojo some meat to cook. One of the wolves came toward Wenebojo belching and looking like he was going to throw up. Another acted the same way and suddenly, out of the mouth of one came a ham and some ribs out of the mouth of another. It is said that wolves have a double stomach, and in this way, they can carry meat home, unspoiled, to their pups.

After that Wenebojo didn't have to leave the camp because the wolves hunted for him and kept him supplied with deer, elk and moose. Wenebojo would prepare the meat and was well off indeed. Toward spring the Old Wolf said they would be leaving and that Wenebojo had enough meat to last until summer. One younger wolf said he thought Wenebojo would be lonesome, so he, the best hunter, would stay with him.

All went well until suddenly the evil manidog [spirits] became jealous of Wenebojo and decided they would take his younger brother away. That night Wenebojo dreamed his brother, while hunting a moose, would meet with misfortune. In the morning, he warned the brother not to cross a lake or stream, even a dry stream bed, without laying a stick across it. When Wolf did not return, Wenebojo feared the worst and set out to search for him. At last, he came to a stream which was rapidly becoming a large river and he saw tracks of a moose and a wolf. Wenebojo realized that Wolf had been careless and neglected to place a stick across the stream.

Desolate, Wenebojo returned to his wigwam. He wanted to find out how his brother had died, so he started out to find him. When he came to a big tree leaning over a stream that emptied into a lake; a bird was sitting in the tree looking down into the water. Wenebojo asked him what he was looking at. The bird said the evil manidog were going to kill Wenebojo's brother and he was waiting for some of the guts to come floating down the stream so he could eat them.

This angered Wenebojo, but he slyly told the bird he would paint it if it told him what it knew. The bird said the manido, who was the chief of the water monsters lived on a big island up the stream, but that he and all the others came out to sun themselves on a warm day. So Wenebojo pretended he would paint the bird, but he really wanted to wring its neck. However, the bird ducked and Wenebojo only hit him on the back of the head, ruffling his feathers. This was the Kingfisher and that was how he got his ruffled crest. From now on, Wenebojo told him, the only way he would get his food would be to sit in a tree all day and wait for it.

Then Wenebojo heard a voice speaking to him. It told him to use the claw of the kingfisher for his arrow and, when he was ready to shoot the water monster, not to shoot at the body, but to look for the place where the shadow was and shoot him there because the shadow and the soul were the same thing.

Wenebojo then traveled up the stream until he came to the island where the chief of the water monsters was lying in the sun. He shot into the side of the shadow. The manido rose up and began to pursue

Wenebojo who ran with all his might, looking for a mountain. He was also pursued by the water, which kept coming higher and higher. At last, he found a tall pine, high up on a mountain, and climbed it. Still the water continued to rise halfway up the tree.

The Sweet Corn Treaty

WENEBOJO AND THE WORLD

Wenebojo, having outwitted the evil manidog by trickery, at last found himself stranded in the pine tree. He crept higher, begging the tree to stretch as tall as it could. Finally, the waters stopped just below Wenebojo's nose. He saw lots of animals swimming around and asked them all, in turn, to dive down and bring up a little earth, so that he and they might live. The loon tried, then the otter and the beaver, but all of them were drowned before they could bring back any earth. Finally, the muskrat went down, but he too passed out as he came to the surface.

"Poor little fellow, " said Wenebojo, "You tried hard." But he saw the muskrat clutching something in his paw, a few grains of sand and a bit of mud. Wenebojo breathed on the muskrat and restored his life, then he took the mud and rolled it in his hands. Soon he had enough for a small island, and he called the other animals to climb out of the water. He sent a huge bird to fly around the island and enlarge it. The bird was gone four days, but Wenebojo said that was not enough and he sent out the eagle to make the land larger. Having created the world, Wenebojo said "Here is where my aunts and uncles and all my relatives can make their home."

Then Wenebojo cut up the body of one of the evil manidog and fed part of it to the woodchuck, who had once saved his life. Into a hollow he put the rest of the food and when some of it turned into oil or fat, Wenebojo told the animals to help themselves. The woodchuck was told to work only in the summertime; in the winter he could rest in a snug den and sleep, and each spring he would have a new coat. Before that, most of the animals had lived on grass and other plants, but now they could eat meat if they wished. The rabbit came and took a little stick with which he touched himself high on the back. The deer and other animals that eat grass all touched themselves on their flanks. Wenebojo told the deer he could eat moss. The bear drank some of the fat, as did the smaller animals who eat meat. All those who sipped the fat were turned into manidog and are the guardian spirits of every Indian who fasts. Wenebojo then named the plants, herbs and roots and instructed the Indians in the use of these plants. Wenebojo's grandmother, Nokomis, also has a lodge somewhere in that land.

Kaishpau Gourneau

WENEBOJO AND THE MOOSE'S SKULL

Wenebojo found the skull of the moose and wondered if there was any meat left inside. He looked inside and up the nose and saw a little piece of meat there. He could crack the moose head open and get the meat, but he didn't do that. Wenebojo wanted that meat badly; so, he thought, "I will become a little snake. Then I will be able to get the meat inside there."

So Wenebojo turned into a little snake. He crawled into the moose's skull and started to eat the meat. It was very good, and he was enjoying it immensely. But before he finished eating it, Wenebojo changed back into his normal shape, and his head got stuck inside the moose skull. He tried and tried to pull the moose skull off his head, but it hurt him too badly. So, he just walked away, thinking that he might be able to get it off another way. Since he was walking and had the moose skull over his head and couldn't see, he didn't get very far before he bumped right into a tree. He touched the tree to see what kind it was, but he couldn't tell. So, he asked, "Brother, what kind of a tree are you?" And the tree answered, "I'm a maple tree."

Then Wenebojo said, "You used to stand close to the river. Is there a river close by?" and the tree said, "No, Wenebojo, there's no river near here."

Wenebojo kept on bumping into all kinds of trees and asking them if there was a river nearby. All the trees answered No. Finally, Wenebojo came to a tree that he didn't know. He said, "Brother, who are you? What kind of tree are you?" The tree answered, "I'm a cedar."

"A cedar!" Wenebojo said, "You always stand at the edge of the river. Is there any river close by?" And the tree answered, "Yes, there is a river close by, Wenebojo. Just follow along my arm until you get to the river."

So Wenebojo felt along the limb of the tree and then kept on going. There was a big high mountain with a river down below and that's where Wenebojo ended up. He walked along the side of the mountain, but his foot slipped, and Wenebojo fell and rolled all the way down to the bottom. When he hit the bottom, the moose skull cracked open and fell apart and he was free of it at last.

Louis Riel

WENEBOJO AND THE CRANBERRIES

Wenebojo was walking along one day by the edge of a lake and saw some highbush cranberries lying in the shallow water. He stuck his hand in the water and tried to get them, but he couldn't. He tried over and over again to get those cranberries. Finally, he gave up trying to stick his hand in the water and instead, he tried to grab them with his mouth by sticking his head in the water. That didn't work either, so he dove down into the water. The water was so shallow that the little rocks in the bottom hurt his face. He jumped out of the water and lay down on his back on the shore holding his face. He opened his eyes and there were the berries hanging above him! He had only seen their reflection in the water. But he was so angry that he tore the berries off the tree and didn't eat any, and he walked away.

WENEBOJO AND THE DANCING GEESE

Wenebojo often took long journeys. On one of these, he happened to hear singing out on a lake, and when he looked to see who was singing, he thought he saw some people dancing. He went toward them, saying how much he would like to join them. Suddenly, he heard some loud laughter and when he looked closer, he realized that what he had thought were dancers were really the reeds swaying in the breeze. He realized that the evil manidog had played a trick on him and he was furious.

He went on along the lake and began to get hungry. He saw some geese swimming a little offshore and thought to himself, "Now, I would like some of those geese to eat."

Wenebojo then gathered some balsam boughs in an old dirty blanket he was carrying and, with this on his shoulder, he called to the goslings and offered to teach them some of the songs he was carrying in his bag. They all crowded into shore, and he told them they must dance just like he did, singing the song he would teach them. He sang "A dance on one leg. Oh, my little brothers!"

And as they danced on one leg, they stretched their necks upward. Then Wenebojo sang, "A dance with my eyes closed, Oh my little brothers!"

And Wenebojo danced and stretched, and the little goslings all did as he did, closing their eyes and stretching themselves. Wenebojo then moved among the foolish goslings and began to break their necks. Just then, the Loon, who had been dancing with the other birds, opened his eyes and immediately began to cry "Look out, we are being killed by Wenebojo!"

By this time, Wenebojo had killed several goslings, but he was so angry with the Loon that he kicked him on the small of the back. That is why the Loon has that peculiar curve to his back.

Wenebojo decided to cook his goslings there on the shore of the lake, so he buried them in the sand, putting their legs up so he could find them when they were cooked. Then he built a fire over them and lay down to sleep. He told his buttocks to keep watch for him and, if anyone came, to wake him, for he did not want his goslings stolen.

While Wenebojo slept, some people came around a bend in the lake. They saw the goslings' legs sticking up in the air and thought that Wenebojo had something good to eat. But they saw Wenebojo stir when his buttocks called him, and they ducked behind some bushes to hide. Wenebojo did not see anything and scolded his buttocks for waking him unnecessarily. Again, the people came out and again the buttocks woke Wenebojo, but since Wenebojo did not see them, he scolded the buttocks once more. The third time the people crept up silently, took the goslings and put the legs back just as they had found them. The buttocks remained silent because they had received a scolding the first two times, they had warned Wenebojo.

When Wenebojo awoke, he was very hungry and started to take out his goslings for. But he could find nothing buried in the ashes. He was furious with his buttocks and decided to punish them by standing over the fire until they were scorched. At last, when the buttocks were black and crisp, Wenebojo tried to walk away, but it was so painful that he could scarcely move.

So, he sat on the top of a steep cliff and slid down, and the sore skin of his buttocks became the lichen. As he walked along, he dragged his bleeding buttocks behind him through some dense shrubs. When he looked back, the shrubs were red from his blood. This, said Wenebojo, will be what the people will use to mix their tobacco-the red willows.

WINDIGO

One winter a newly married couple went hunting with the other people. When they moved to the hunting grounds a child was born to them. One day, as they were gazing at him in his cradleboard and talking to him, the child spoke to them. They were very surprised because he was too young to talk. "Where is that manidogisik (Sky Spirit)?" asked the baby. "They say he is very powerful and someday I am going to visit him."

His mother grabbed him and said, "You should not talk about that manido that way."

A few nights later, they fell asleep again with the baby in his cradleboard between them. In the middle of the night the mother awoke and discovered that her baby was gone. She woke her husband, and he got up, started a fire and looked all over the wigwam for the baby. They searched the neighbor's wigwam but could not find it. They lit birchbark torches and searched the community looking for tracks. At last, they found some tiny tracks leading down to the lake. Halfway down to the lake, they found the cradleboard and they knew then the baby himself had made the tracks, had crawled out of his cradleboard and was headed for the manido. The tracks leading from the cradle down to the lake were large, far bigger than human feet, and the parents realized that their child had turned into a windigo, the terrible ice monster who could eat people. They could see his tracks where he had walked across the lake.

The manidogisik had fifty smaller manidog or little people to protect him. When one of these manidog threw a rock, it was a bolt of lightning. As the windigo approached, the manidog heard him coming and ran out to meet him and began to fight. Finally, they knocked him down with a bolt of lightning. The windigo fell dead with a noise like a big tree falling. As he lay there, he looked like a big Indian, but when the people started to chop him up, he was a huge block of ice. They melted down the pieces and found, in the middle of the body, a tiny infant about six inches long with a hole in his head where the manidog had hit him. This was the baby who had turned into a windigo. If the manidog had not killed it, the windigo would have eaten up the whole village.

Li Bangs (Frybread)

2 cups flour
1 tablespoon sugar
1 teaspoon salt
1 packet yeast
1 cup warm water

Combine yeast and warm water to activate and let sit for 5 to 10 minutes. Combine dry ingredients and add half the activated yeast, then mix. Add small amounts of the yeast until the mixture forms a dough-like consistency. Sprinkle flour on a flat surface and roll out the dough. You can pull off pieces of dough and hand-press into shape, or else roll out and cut into shape (about 3" to 4" in size). Place into oil and fry until golden brown.

Frybread can be enjoyed with a variety of meals.

ANOTHER WINDIGO STORY

The villagers realized a windigo was coming when they saw a kettle swinging back and forth over the fire. No one was brave enough or strong enough to challenge this ice creature. After they had sent for a wise old grandmother who lived at the edge of the village, the little grandchild, hearing the old woman say she was without power to do anything, asked what was wrong. While the people moaned that they would all die, the little girl asked for two sticks of peeled sumac as long as her arms. She took these home with her while the frightened villagers huddled together.

That night it turned bitterly cold. The child told her grandmother to melt a kettle of tallow over the fire. As the people watched, trees began to crack open, and the river froze solid. All this was caused by the windigo, as tall as a white pine tree, coming over the hill.

With a sumac stick gripped in each hand, the little girl ran out to meet him. She had two dogs which ran ahead of her and killed the windigo's dog. But still the windigo came on. The little girl got bigger and bigger until when they met, she was as big as the windigo himself. With one sumac stick, she knocked him down and with the other she crushed his skull-the sticks had turned to copper. After she killed the windigo, the little girl swallowed the hot tallow and gradually grew smaller until she was herself again.

Everyone rushed over to the windigo and began to chop him up. He was made of ice, but in the center, they found the body of a man with his skull crushed in. The people were very thankful and gave the little girl everything she wanted.

THE UNDERWATER PANTHER

There once was a big lake where Indians lived all around it. In the middle of the lake, there was a big island of mud, which made it impossible just to paddle straight across. So, if someone in one village wanted to go to the one on the opposite side, they would have to paddle all around the edge of the lake. They stayed away from the island of mud because a bad manido.

One day, one of the villages was holding a dance, and the people from the other side of the lake started out in their canoes, coming around the edge of the lake. Two women who were going started out late, after everyone else had gone. The two women were sisters-in-law and one of them was rather foolish. She was steering the canoe and headed straight across the lake to the island of mud. The other warned her not to do it, but it didn't do any good. The first girl carried a little cedar paddle with her but did not use it for paddling. She carried it everywhere with her. As they got to the middle of the lake, they started to cross the island of mud, and in the center of the mud they saw a hole of clear water. The water was swirling around like a whirlpool, and as they started to cross that bit of open water, a panther came out and twitched his tail across the boat and tried to turn it over. The girl picked up her little cedar paddle and hit the panther's tail with it. As she hit it, she said, "Thunder is striking you." The paddle cut off the panther's tail where she had hit it, and the end dropped into the boat. It was a solid piece of copper about two inches thick. The panther ran away through the mud, and they laughed hard. One girl said, "I guess I scared him. He won't bother us again." When they got across, the girl gave the piece of copper to her father. The copper tail of the underwater panther had magical powers. Everyone wanted a little piece of the tail to carry for luck in hunting and fishing and people would give her father a blanket for a tiny piece of that copper. Her family got rich from the tail of the underwater panther.

Albert Lee Ferris

THE MINK AND THE FISH

Mink found a live pike on the lake shore. He told the pike, "Pike, the Muskie is calling you all kinds of names." "What is he calling me?" asked Pike. Mink answered, "He says you're wall-eyed." Pike did not like to be called names and said, "Well, he's got teeth like a saw blade and a long-plated face. He's not pretty either."

There was a muskie nearby, and Mink told him what Pike had said about him. Mink went back and forth, back and forth, getting Muskie and Pike mad at one another. Finally, Pike and Muskie had a big fight and Mink acted as referee. Muskie and Pike ended up killing each other in the fight, so Mink had the last laugh on them.

Mink got a big kettle and boiled and dried the meat. Then he lay down to rest. He was taking life easy. He had the fish eggs, which were his favorite, all together next to him and all he had to do was open his eyes and stick out his tongue out to eat them. Finally, he dozed off.

Some Indians came by in their canoes and saw Mink lying there with all those fish. They came ashore and picked up all the fish and put them in their canoes. Where Mink had all the fish eggs right next to him, they put rocks there. Then they went away.

When Mink woke up, he reached with his tongue for the fish eggs, but instead there was only rocks and stones which broke his teeth. He realized they'd played a trick on him, and he just walked away.

THE HELLDIVER AND THE SPIRIT OF WINTER

Every winter, the birds fly south. One winter, a helldiver (also called a grebe) told all of the other birds that he would stay for the winter to take care of two of his friends who had been injured and couldn't fly south. Both of his friends, a whooping crane and mallard duck, had broken wings. To feed them, he got fish by diving through a hole in the ice. But the Spirit of Winter got jealous of his success at fishing and froze the water after the helldiver had dived through his hole below the ice. But the helldiver swam to shore where there were a lot of reeds and bulrushes. He pulled one of them down through the ice with his bill to make a hole in the ice and so he got out and flew home.

When he got home, he saw that someone was peeking in the door of his wigwam. It was the Spirit of Winter, who did not like him and who was trying to freeze him out. The helldiver got a big fire going, but it was still cold in the wigwam because the Spirit of Winter was right there making it cold. But the helldiver tricked the Spirit of Winter by mopping his face with a handkerchief and saying, "Gee, but it's hot in here!" The Spirit of Winter thought the fire was hot enough to melt him, so he ran away.

One day the helldiver decided to have a feast. He got some wild rice and sent a duck to invite the Spirit of Winter, but it was so cold that the duck froze to death before he got there. Then he sent Partridge with the invitation. She got very cold too, but she dove under the snow to warm up and then went on again. She reached the Spirit of Winter and invited him to the hell-diver's feast.

When the Spirit of Winter came to the feast, it was like a blizzard coming in the door of the wigwam. He had icicles on his nose and face. Hell-diver built the fire higher and higher, and it began to get warm inside the wigwam. The icicles began to melt on the Spirit of Winter's face. He was getting awfully warm, but he liked the wild rice that helldiver had at his feast and wanted to keep eating.

Hell-diver said, "Whew! It's very warm in here. It must be spring already." The Spirit of Winter got scared and grabbed his blanket and ran out of the wigwam. With his fire, Helldiver had brought the spring and outside, things were already melting and there were just patches of snow here and there. The Spirit of Winter had a hard time getting back to his home in the north, where there is always snow.

Fall Ricing on Lower Rice Lake

THE STORY OF REDFEATHER

There once was a little boy called Redfeather who lived with his great-grandfather. His great-grandfather taught him to shoot with his bow and arrows. They lived in a village near a great big frog-meadow. The old grandfather told Redfeather stories about the different ways of creatures.

Springtime came, and in the evenings the old lady frogs would croak and sharpen their knives to butcher the crawfish. That is the noise they make. Every day Redfeather would take his bow and arrow and kill all the frogs he could get and the crawfish too. One day a heron came along and told Redfeather that she would give him her best feather if he would leave the frogs alone. She told him that she had a nest of babies to feed and that he was wasting her food by killing all the frogs and crayfish. Redfeather said, "Ha! I don't want your old dirty feathers. You can keep your feathers and leave me alone. I can do what I want."

So, the birds met together to figure out what to do about Redfeather, who was making life difficult for so many of them. Near Redfeathers's village there was an island with some large trees on it, and on this island lived a very old and very wise owl. Every evening Redfeather would go out and refuse to come in to bed and run around and be noisy. The crane and the owl and other birds all complained about him because he scared away all the rabbits and small birds. They said he must be punished. The crane said that she was starving because he killed the frogs and the birds. No one could live in peace.

On evening, the owl perched himself on a tree close to Redfeather's wigwam, and said, "Hoo Hoo!"

Redfeather's great-grandfather said to him, "Redfeather, come in, don't you hear that owl calling?" But Redfeather said, "I'll get the biggest arrow and shoot him." Grandfather said, "The owl has large ears, and he can put rabbits and other food in them. He might catch you too. You'd better come in and go to sleep." But Redfeather disobeyed his grandfather and went out and shot at the owl. He missed, and while he was out looking for the arrow, the owl swooped down and picked him up and stuck him in his ears and flew off with him. The owl flew across the lake to his island, and up into an old oak tree where the nest of baby owls was.

He put Redfeather down there, and told his babies, "When you get big enough to eat meat, you shall eat Redfeather." The little owls were quite excited at this. Then the owl flew away. The next day, the owl called to the crane and the other birds and said, "When your babies are old enough, we'll have a feast of Redfeather. I have him imprisoned in my oak tree." So Redfeather was kept a prisoner, and he cried, but he couldn't get down.

Back in the village, all the Indians knew Redfeather was lost. His great-grandfather asked all the living beings to help him find Redfeather and at last they found him a prisoner in the owl's tree. The spirits told the great-grandfather to give a great feast and ask the owl to return Redfeather. His great-grandfather gave a huge feast, and Redfeather was returned to his great-grandfather. Redfeather also promised that he would never again misuse the food that Wenebojo had made for the birds.

Man Who Knows How To Hunt

WHY THE PORCUPINE HAS QUILLS

Long, long ago, the Porcupines had no quills. One day, a Porcupine was out in the woods. A Bear came along and would have eaten Porcupine, but he managed to get up a tree where the Bear couldn't get him.

The next day Porcupine was out again, and he went underneath a hawthorn tree, and he noticed how the thorns pricked him. He broke some branches off and put them on his back, then he went into the woods. Along came Bear and he jumped on Porcupine, who just curled himself up. The Bear just left him alone because the thorns pricked him so much.

Wenebojo was watching them. He called to Porcupine and asked, "How did you think of that trick?" Porcupine told him that he was in danger when Bear was around. Then Wenebojo took some thorns and peeled the bark off of them until they were all white. Then he got some clay and put it all over Porcupine's back and stuck the thorns in it. Wenebojo used his magic to make it into a proper skin, and told Porcupine come with him into the woods. When they got there, Wenebojo hid behind a tree. Wolf came along and saw Porcupine and jumped on him, but the new quills pricked at him, and Wolf ran away. Bear was also afraid of the quills and Porcupine was safe. That is why Porcupines have quills.

WHY THE BUFFALO HAS A HUMP

Long ago, the Buffalo didn't have any hump. In the summer he would race across the prairies for fun, and the Foxes would run in front of him and tell all the little animals to get out of the way because the Buffalo was coming. They didn't know that Wenebojo was watching them.

So, the Buffalo raced across the prairies. There were little birds nesting on the ground and the Buffalo raced over them and tramped their nests. The little birds cried out and told him not to go near their nests, but Buffalo didn't listen to them and ran right over them.

The birds were sad and kept crying about their spoiled nests. Wenebojo heard them and he ran ahead of the Buffalo and Foxes and stopped them. With a stick, he hit the Buffalo on the shoulders, and the Buffalo hung his head and humped up his shoulders because he was afraid that Wenebojo would hit him with the stick again. But Wenebojo just said "You should be ashamed. You will always have a hump on your shoulder, and always carry your head low because of your shame." The Foxes were also afraid of Wenebojo and ran away and dug holes in the ground where they hid. And Wenebojo said to them "And you, Foxes, you will always live in the cold ground for hurting the birds." And that is why the Buffalo have humps, and why the Foxes have holes in the ground for their homes.

WENEBOJO MADE A HOUSE FOR TORTOISE

Long ago, when the world was young, there were only two tortoises. They didn't have any shells or houses on their backs as we know them today. They were all soft. In the woods, the strong animals hunt the weaker animals, and Otter planned on eating the Tortoise. One day, Tortoise wanted to go on land to take a walk, but he couldn't run very fast, so he looked around to see if any of the other animals were there. As he looked around, he saw Otter coming so Tortoise turned around and crawled under a piece of bark and drew his head, legs, and tail in and Otter didn't see him. When Otter was gone, Tortoise went back to the pond where he lived. But he didn't know that Wenebojo was watching him and saw how he had saved himself from Otter.

One morning Wenebojo was out fishing, he asked Tortoise where there were lots of fish. He said, "If you tell me, I'll give you a sturdy house that you can carry on your back." As soon as the Tortoise heard this, he dived down and looked for fish and found a lot and then he came back and told Wenebojo where they were. Wenebojo thanked him and got out of his canoe and asked Tortoise to come up on land with him. There Wenebojo found a piece of bark and put it on the Tortoise's back and got another piece and put it on his stomach. Then they watched for Otter to come. When they saw him coming, Tortoise went out on the path and pretended that he didn't see Otter coming. When Otter saw Tortoise, he jumped on him so he could eat him, but Tortoise drew his head, legs, and tail into the new shell and was safe. After Otter went away, Wenebojo told Tortoise that "From this day forth, every

Tortoise shall carry his shell, or house, along wherever he goes."

Auguste

THE MAGIC POTS

A long time ago, a very old woman lived in an Ojibwe village. Besides the wigwam she lived in, she also had a separate bark house where she kept five beautiful pots on a shelf. These pots were magical and weren't supposed to be used for cooking or anything. Instead, the old woman kept them there so the other women of the village could come look at them and get ideas and go home and make their own pots to use. No one could make pottery without the inspiration of the magic pots and, to keep them safe, no one but the old woman was allowed to touch the pots.

One year, everyone went out at the same time to pick berries, and the old woman went along too. In the village, five little girls were left behind to tend to their chores. They quickly gathered firewood and did all of their other chores and then got together to play. Out of curiosity, the girls went to the old woman's bark house where she kept the magic pots so they could get a look at how beautiful they were. But that wasn't enough for them, and they got the pots down off their shelf and took them outside and played with them, despite the fact that the old woman had forbidden anyone to touch the pots.

As the girls were playing, a wolf appeared. The girls were frightened and got up to run into one of the houses to get away from the wolf. As they ran, one of them fell over the birchbark sheet they used to cover the ground under the pots, and instantly there was a noise like thunder. When the wolf was gone, the girls came out and found that all of the pots had all been shattered into tiny pieces.

When the old woman returned and found out what had happened, she found the five girls and told them what they had done. As soon as she told them, a magic thing happened, and the disobedient girls were changed into five black crows which flew away, cawing.

Without the magic pots, the women no longer knew how to make pottery, and that is why the Ojibwe no longer make pots. But the crows live on and in summer you can see them in some tall tree, uttering a mournful caw, caw.

The Jingle Dress
(ziibaaska'iganagooday)

HOW THE INDIANS GOT MAPLE SUGAR

One day Wenebojo was standing under a maple tree. Suddenly it began to rain maple syrup-not sap-right on top of him. Wenebojo got a birchbark tray and held it out to catch the syrup. He said to himself: "This is too easy for the Indians to have the syrup just rain down like this." So, he threw the syrup away and decided that before they could have the syrup, the Indians would have to give a feast, offer tobacco, speak to the manido, and put out some birchbark trays.

Nokomis, the grandmother of Wenehojo, showed him how to insert a small piece of wood into each maple tree so the sap could run down into the vessels beneath. When Manabush tested it, it was thick and sweet. He told his grandmother it would never do to give the Indians the syrup without making them work for it. He climbed to the top of one of the maples, scattered rain over all the trees, dissolving the sugar as it flowed into the birchbark vessels. Now the Indians have to cut wood, make vessels, collect the sap and boil it for a long time. If they want the maple syrup, they have to work hard for it.

SKUNK WOMAN

Once there was an Ojibwe man who was a good hunter, but he had a very bad temper. He would always yell at his brothers or the other men whenever they made a mistake. Soon nobody wanted to go hunting with him anymore.

Eventually the hunter got married, so he and his wife went off on their own. She was a hard-working woman, and he was a good provider, so they were happy together by themselves. But one day he lost his temper with her too. She made a lot of noise while he was trying to trap beaver and spoiled his trapping, so he really yelled at her a lot. His wife ran back to the wigwam and took their son. She sang a song, but I don't know how it goes. It had the same idea as "Your father doesn't want us anymore; your father doesn't want us anymore." And she went away.

That night when the hunter came back, he saw that they were gone. And he felt bad, because he knew he shouldn't have lost his temper. So, he decided to follow them. He found their tracks in the mud and hurried after his wife and son. He was good at tracking, and he thought he could catch up to them soon. So, he hurried along, but as he went, he started to see that something was happening to their footprints. They didn't look like moccasin prints anymore. They were starting to look like skunk footprints.

Suddenly the hunter arrived in a marsh. The footprints ended, and he was surrounded by skunks. There was nothing there but skunks. He couldn't tell which ones were his wife and child. So, he had to go back home.

After a while the hunter remarried, and he always told his children, "Don't eat skunks. You must never eat skunks, because your brother is a skunk now. You might be eating your brother." And they never did. That family never ate skunks again. And as for the hunter, he changed his attitude, and he didn't yell at his family members anymore.

Grass Dancing

SHAWONDASEE AND THE GOLDEN GIRL

Shawondasee, the South Wind, was much gentler than his brothers of the East, West, and North. He liked to go softly and enjoy the beauty of the world. He was also rather shy.

So, one spring day when he looked across the meadow and saw a lovely maiden dressed in green, with amazing hair as yellow as the sun, he didn't dare rush to her side. He just admired her from afar, and that night went to sleep promising himself, "Tomorrow I'll go introduce myself."

The next day Shawondasee saw her again, but he hesitated. "I mustn't be too bold. I don't want to scare her." Each night he went to bed sighing over her beauty and hoping that the next day he'd have courage to ask her to marry him.

But one morning he could hardly see her bright hair. Had she pulled her green shawl over her head? If she was upset about something, this was not the day to visit her.

And the next day he found that he had waited too long. Her hair had turned completely white, like an old woman! Shawondesee sighed mightily with grief and disappointment. The air filled with silvery puffs like thistledown, and when he looked again, she had disappeared.

Poor Shawondasee! He had fallen in love with Dandelion!

OLD MAN REMAKES THE WORLD

THE sun was just sinking behind the hills when we started for War Eagle's lodge.

"To-morrow will be a fine day," said Other-person, "for grandfather says that a red sky is always the sun's promise of fine weather, and the sun cannot lie."

"Yes," said Bluebird, "and he said that when this moon was new it travelled well south for this time of year and its points were up. That means fine, warm weather."

"I wish I knew as much as grandfather," said Fine-bow with pride.

The pipe was laid aside at once upon our entering the lodge and the old warrior said:

"I have told you that Old man taught the animals and the birds all they know. He made them and therefore knew just what each would have to understand in order to make his living. They have never forgotten anything he told them -- even to this day. Their grandfathers told the young ones what they had been told, just as I am telling you the things you should know. Be like the birds and animals -- tell your children and grandchildren what I have told you, that our people may always know how things were made, and why strange things are true.

"Yes -- Old-man taught the Beaver how to build his dams to make the water deeper; taught the Squirrel to plant the pine-nut so that another tree might grow and have nuts for his children; told the Bear to go to sleep in the winter, when the snow made hard travelling for his short legs -- told him to sleep, and promised him that he would need no meat while he slept. All winter long the Bear sleeps and eats nothing, because old man told him that he could. He sleeps so much in the winter that he spends most of his time in summer hunting.

"It was Old-man who showed the Owl how to hunt at night and it was Old-man that taught the Weasel all his wonderful ways -- his bloodthirsty ways -- for the Weasel is the bravest of the animal-people, considering his size. He taught the Beaver one strange thing that you have noticed, and that is to lay sticks on the creek-bottoms, so that they will stay there as long as he wants them to.

"Whenever the animal-people got into trouble they always sought Old-man and told him about it. All were busy working and making a living, when one day it commenced to rain. That was nothing, of course, but it didn't stop as it had always done before. No, it kept right on raining until the rivers overran their banks, and the water chased the Weasel out of his hole in the ground. Yes, and it found the Rabbit's hiding-place and made him leave it. It crept into the lodge of the Wolf at night and frightened his wife and children. It poured into the den of the Bear among the rocks, and he had to move. It crawled under the logs in the forest and found the Mice-people. Out it went to the plains and chased them out of their homes in the buffalo skulls. At last, the Beavers' dams broke under the strain and that made everything worse. It was bad -- very bad, indeed. Everybody except the fish-people were frightened and all went to find Old-man that they might tell him what had happened. Finally, they found his fire, far up on a timbered bench, and they said that they wanted a council right away.

"It was a strange sight to see the Eagle sitting next to the Grouse; the Rabbit sitting close to the Lynx; the Mouse right under the very nose of the Bobcat, and the tiny Hummingbird talking to the Hawk in a whisper, as though they had always been great friends. All about Old-man's fire they sat and whispered or talked in signs. Even the Deer spoke to the Mountain-lion, and the Antelope told the Wolf that he was glad to see him, because fear had made them all friends.

"The whispering and the sign-making stopped when Old-man raised his hand-like that" (here War Eagle raised his hand with the palm outward) -- "and asked them what was troubling them.

"The Bear spoke first, of course, and told how the water had made him move his camp. He said all the animal-people were moving their homes, and he was afraid they would be unable to find good camping-places, because of the water. Then the Beaver spoke, because he is wise, and all the forest-people know it. He said his dams would not hold back the water that came against them; that the whole world was a lake, and that he thought they were on an island. He said he could live in the water longer than most people, but that as far as he could see they would all die except, perhaps, the fish-people, who stayed in the water all the time, anyhow. He said he couldn't think of a thing to do -- then he sat down and the sign-talking and whispering commenced again.

"Old-man smoked a long time -- smoked and thought hard. Finally, he grabbed his magic stone axe, and began to sing his war song. Then the rest knew he had made up his mind and knew what he would do.

Swow! he struck a mighty pine-tree a blow, and it fell down. Swow! down went another and another, until he had ten times ten of the longest, straightest, and largest trees in all the world lying side by side before him. Then Old man chopped off the limbs, and with the aid of magic rolled the great logs tight together. With withes of willow that he told the Beaver to cut for him, he bound the logs fast together until they were all as one. It was a monstrous raft that old man had built, as he sang his song in the darkness. At last, he cried, 'Ho! everybody hurries and sit on this raft I have made'; and they did hurry.

"It was not long till the water had reached the logs; then it crept in between them, and finally it went on past the raft and off into the forest, looking for more trouble.

"By and by the raft began to groan, and the willow withes squeaked and cried out as though ghost-people were crying in the night. That was when the great logs began to tremble as the water lifted them from the ground. Rain was falling -- night was there, and fear made cowards of the bravest on the raft. All through the forest there were bad noises -- noises that make the heart cold -- as the raft bumped against great trees rising from the earth that they were leaving forever.

"Higher and higher went the raft; higher than the bushes; higher than the limbs on the trees; higher than the Woodpecker's nest; higher than the treetops, and even higher than the mountains. Then the world was no more, for the water had whipped the land in the war it made against it.

"Day came, and still the rain was falling. Night returned, and yet the rain came down. For many days and nights, they drifted in the falling rain; whirling and twisting about while the water played with the great raft, as a Bear would play with a Mouse. It was bad, and they were all afraid -- even Old-man himself was scared.

"At last, the sun came but there was no land. All was water. The water was the world. It reached even to the sky and touched it all about the edges. All were hungry, and some of them were grumbling, too. There are always grumblers when there is great trouble, but they are not the ones who become great chiefs -- ever.

"Old man sat in the middle of the raft and thought. He knew that something must be done, but he didn't know what. Finally, he said: 'Ho! Chipmunk, bring me the Spotted Loon. Tell him I want him.'

"The Chipmunk found the Spotted Loon and told him that Old-man wanted him, so the Loon went to where Old-man sat. When he got there, Old man said:

"'Spotted Loon you are a great diver. Nobody can dive as you can. I made you that way and I know. If you will dive and swim down to the world, I think you might bring me some of the dirt that it is made of -- then I am sure I can make another world.'

"'It is too deep, this water,' replied the Loon, 'I am afraid I shall drown.'

"'Well, what if you do?' said Old man. 'I gave your life, and if you lose it this way, I will return it to you. You shall live again!'

"'All right, Old-man,' he answered, 'I am willing to try'; so he waddled to the edge of the raft. He is a poor walker -- the Loon, and you know I told you why.

It was all because Old-man kicked him in the back the night he painted all the Duck-people.

"Down went the Spotted Loon, and long he stayed beneath the water. All waited and watched, and longed for good luck, but when he came to the top, he was dead. Everybody groaned -- all felt badly, I can tell you, as Old-man laid the dead Loon on the logs. The Loon's wife was crying, but Old-man told her to shut up and she did.

"Then Old-man blew his own breath into the Loon's bill, and he came back to life.

"'What did you see, Brother Loon?' asked Old-man, while everybody crowded as close as he could.

"'Nothing but water,' answered the Loon, 'we shall all die here, I cannot reach the world by swimming. My heart stops working.'

"There were many brave ones on the raft, and the Otter tried to reach the world by diving; and the Beaver, and the Gray Goose, and the Gray Goose's wife; but all died in trying, and all were given a new life by Old-man. Things were bad and getting worse. Everybody was cross, and all wondered what Old-man would do next, when somebody laughed.

"All turned to see what there could be to laugh at, at such a time, and Old-man turned about just in time to see the Muskrat bid good-by to his wife -- that was what they were laughing at. But he paid no attention to Old-man or the rest and slipped from the raft to the water. Flip! -- his tail cut the water like a knife, and he was gone. Some laughed again, but all wondered at his daring, and waited with little hope in their hearts; for the Muskrat wasn't very great, they thought.

"He was gone longer than the Loon, longer than the Beaver, longer than the Otter or the Gray Goose or his wife, but when he came to the surface of the water, he was dead.

"Old-man brought Muskrat back to life and asked him what he had seen on his journey. Muskrat said: 'I saw trees, Old-man, but I died before I got to them.'

"Old-man told him he was brave. He said his people should forever be great if he succeeded in bringing some dirt to the raft; so just as soon as the Muskrat was rested, he dove again.

"When he came up, he was dead, but clinched in his tiny hand Old-man found some dirt -- not much, but a little. A second time Old-man gave the Muskrat his breath, and told him that he must go once more, and bring dirt. He said there was not quite enough in the first lot, so after resting a while the Muskrat tried a third time and a third time, he died but brought up a little more dirt.

"Everybody on the raft was anxious now, and they were all crowding about Old-man; but he told them to stand back, and they did. Then he blew his breath in Muskrat's mouth a third time, and a third time he lived and joined his wife.

"Old-man then dried the dirt in his hands, rubbing it slowly and singing a queer song. Finally, it was dry; then he settled the hand that held the dirt in the water slowly, until the water touched the dirt. The dry dirt began to whirl about and then Old-man blew upon it. Hard he blew and waved his hands, and the dirt began to grow in size right before their eyes. Old-man kept blowing and waving his hands until the dirt became real land, and the trees began to grow. So large it grew that none could see across it. Then he stopped his blowing and sang some more. Everybody wanted to get off the raft, but Old-man said 'no.'

"'Come here, Wolf,' he said, and the Wolf came to him.

"'You are swift of foot and brave. Run around this land I have made, that I may know how large it is.'

"The Wolf started, and it took him half a year to get back to the raft. He was very poor from much running, too, but Old-man said the world wasn't big enough yet, so he blew some more, and again sent the Wolf out to run around the land. He never came back -- no, the Old-man had made it so big that the Wolf died of old age before he got back to the raft. Then all the people went out upon the land to make their living, and they were happy, there, too.

"After they had been on the land for a long time Old-man said: 'Now I shall make a man and a woman, for I am lonesome living with you people. He took two or three handfuls of mud from the world he had made and molded both a man and a woman. Then he set them side by side and breathed upon them. They lived! -- and he made them very strong and healthy -- very beautiful to look upon. Chippewas, he called these people, and they lived happily on that world until a white man saw an Eagle sailing over the land and came to look about. He stole the woman -- that white man did; and that is where all the tribes came from that we know to-day. None are pure of blood but the two humans he made of clay, and their own children. And they are the Chippewas!

"That is a long story and now you must hurry to bed. To-morrow night I will tell you another story -- Ho!"

Eli Guardipee

HOW THE MAN FOUND HIS MATE

Each tribe has its own stories. Most of them deal with the same subjects, differing only in immaterial particulars.

Instead of squirrels in the timber, the Black-feet are sure they were prairie-dogs that Old-man roasted that time when he made the mountain-lion long and lean. The Chippewas and Crees insist that they were squirrels that were cooked and eaten, but one tribe is essentially a forest-people and the other lives on the plains -- hence the difference.

Some tribes will not wear the feathers of the owl, nor will they have anything to do with that bird, while others use his feathers freely.

The forest Indian wears the soft-soled moccasin, while his brother of the plains covers the bottoms of his footwear with rawhide, because of the cactus and prickly-pear, most likely.

The door of the lodge of the forest Indian reaches to the ground, but the plains Indian makes his lodge skin to reach all about the circle at the bottom, because of the wind.

One night in War Eagle's lodge, Other-person asked: "Why don't the Bear have a tail, grandfather?"

War Eagle laughed and said: "Our people do not know why, but we believe he was made that way at the beginning, although I have heard men of other tribes say that the Bear lost his tail while fishing.

"I don't know how true it is, but I have been told that a long time ago the Bear was fishing in the winter, and the Fox asked him if he had any luck.

"'No,' replied the Bear, 'I can't catch a fish.'

"'Well,' said the Fox, 'if you will stick your long tail down through this hole in the ice, and sit very still, I am sure you will catch a fish.'

"So, the Bear stuck his tail through the hole in the ice, and the Fox told him to sit still, till he called him; then the Fox went off, pretending to hunt along the bank. It was mighty cold weather, and the water froze everything about the Bear's tail, yet he sat still, waiting for the Fox to call him. Yes, the Bear sat so still and so long that his tail was frozen in the ice, but he didn't know it. When the Fox thought it was time, he called:

"'Hey, Bear, come here quick -- quick! I have a Rabbit in this hole, and I want you to help me dig him out.' Ho! The Bear tried to get up, but he couldn't.

"'Hey, Bear, come here -- there are two Rabbits in this hole,' called the Fox.

"The Bear pulled so hard to get away from the ice, that he broke his tail off short to his body. Then the Fox ran away laughing at the Bear.

"I hardly believe that story, but once I heard an old man who visited my father from the country far east of here, tell it. I remembered it. But I can't say that I know it is true, as I can the others.

"When I told you the story of how Old-man made the world over, after the water had made its war upon it, I told you how the first man and woman were made. There is another story of how the first man found his wife, and I will tell you that.

"After Old-man had made a man to look like himself, he left him to live with the Wolves, and went away. The man had a hard time of it, with no clothes to keep him warm, and no wife to help him, so he went out looking for Old-man.

"It took the man a long time to find Old-man's lodge, but as soon as he got there, he went right in and said:

"'Old-man, you have made me and left me to live with the Wolf-people. I don't like them at all. They give me scraps of meat to eat and won't build a fire. They have wives,

but I don't want a Wolf-woman. I think you should take better care of me.'

"'Well,' replied Old-man, 'I was just waiting for you to come to see me. I have things fixed for you. You go down this river until you come to a steep hillside. There you will see a lodge. Then I will leave you to do the rest. Go!'

"The man started and travelled all that day. When night came, he camped and ate some berries that grew near the river. The next morning, he started down the river again, looking for the steep hillside and the lodge. Just before sundown, the man saw a fine lodge near a steep hillside, and he knew that was the lodge he was looking for; so, he crossed the river and went into the lodge.

"Sitting by the fire inside, was a woman. She was dressed in buckskin clothes and was cooking some meat that smelled good to the man, but when she saw him without any clothes, she pushed him out of the lodge, and dropped the door.

"Things didn't look very good to that man, I tell you, but to get even with the woman, he went up on the steep hillside and commenced to roll big rocks down upon her lodge. He kept this up until one of the largest rocks knocked down the lodge, and the woman ran out, crying.

"When the man heard the woman crying, it made him sorry, and he ran down the hill to her. She sat down on the ground, and the man ran to where she was and said:

"'I am sorry I made you cry, woman. I will help you fix your lodge. I will stay with you, if you will only let me.'

"That pleased the woman, and she showed the man how to fix up the lodge and gather some wood for the fire. Then she let him come inside and eat. Finally, she made him some clothes, and they got along very well, after that.

"That is how the man found his wife -- Ho!"

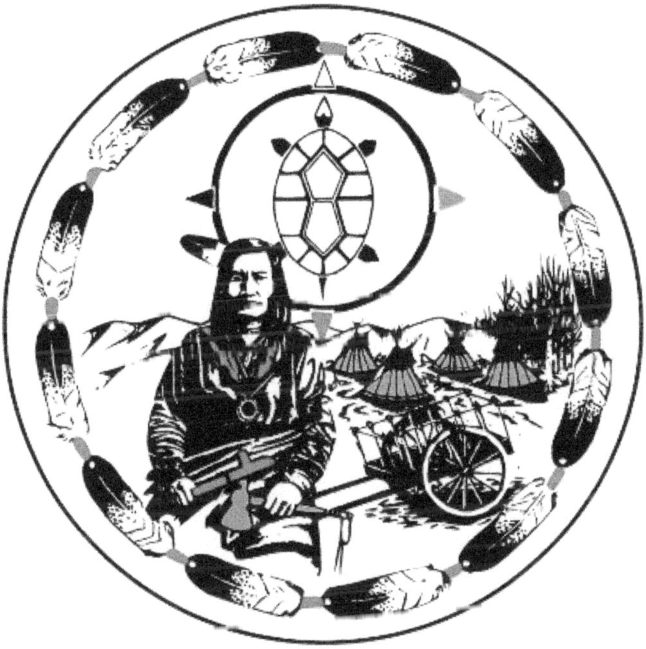

Made in the USA
Columbia, SC
13 February 2024